Unseen

Edward Oak-Rhind

Preface.

I've often wondered what it would be like to be invisible. And to be invisible from the point of view of a normal, ordinary man. Not a mad scientist like all those other invisible men in books and movies. It was a question me and my mates would ponder at school. Would you rather be invisible, or able to fly? I'd always choose invisibility. It was a hill I was prepared to die on and despite the ludicrous nature of this hypothetical scenario, it was one we all cared about and heated arguments would ensue.

And now, having written this book and explored what it would really be like to be unseen, maybe having the power of flight would be a safer option after all. If only I could time travel, then I could go back and change my position.

~~All~~ Most of the events in this book are taken from my imagination. Any similarities to persons living or dead are purely coincidental.

Edward Oak-Rhind

March 2024

For Jacki, Caitlin, Oliver, Jack, Ian, Mary and Django.

Familia super omnia. Always.

One

There was near silence in the wood-panelled boardroom as the two men sat, wordlessly facing each other. The air was thick with tension. Negotiations hadn't been easy, days of bartering had come to this. The clock on the wall ticked noisily. It seemed to get louder as the seconds slowly crawled by. Eric Curtis swallowed hard. He looked at the document in front of him, knowing that he could simply sign his name and it would be done and he would be free to leave. He didn't blink. He looked at the man opposite him, holding out a Mont Blanc pen, motioning towards the document, imploring him to agree to the terms.

Outside, a car alarm sounded, and in the distance a police siren wailed as it sped to some unseen emergency. Eric sighed. It was getting dark. He thought to himself "enough now, it's time to move on". He looked at the clock again. Almost 5pm. If he didn't sign now they'd have to do this all again tomorrow. And he couldn't face another day of this.

He signed his name with a flourish and the deal was done. He slumped in his chair. Eric had been beaten into submission because he didn't want to be late home for his spaghetti Bolognese.

A three percent price increase for his customer, and a one percent increase for his staff. A terrible deal for everyone except the call centre company he had been employed by for twenty years. As usual. Kenny Sinclair, his arch nemesis and the Financial Director of the outsourcing company Eric worked for had triumphed by virtue of just waiting for Eric to give up. As he always did.

What happens when no one can see you? *"Life is a rollercoaster"*. That wasn't true. For Eric Curtis, it was a treadmill, with the speed set to "plod endlessly until you die of boredom". These annual price and salary rise negotiations were the most excitement Eric had at work, and every year he vowed that they would be the last. This time next year, he promised himself as he climbed into his car, he'd be working somewhere that would inspire and motivate him. Next year.

Eric had just turned fifty. He had a decent job running a relatively successful call centre in West London, and had always assumed he was ambling along quite steadily without ever actually being truly happy: two kids, a dog, a wife, a nice house in a nice town with a nice little garden, two nice cars, a motorbike and a mortgage that wasn't killing him.
 It had a nice supermarket and a not-so-nice one, a petrol station and ten thousand houses with ten

thousand satellite dishes bolted onto the side. It had the ubiquitous gang of feral kids with acne and terrible hair who'd wander the streets with their hands permanently stuffed down their grey jogging bottoms. It had a dozen charity shops, a park, a Turkish barber, good broadband speeds and a railway station where trains stopped every hour and didn't go anywhere particularly helpful or interesting.

Welcome to Little Boring, England. It was nice. No more, no less.

Eric would take the kids to their various sports at weekends, He'd occasionally go the pub to watch football with his neighbours who nowadays passed as his friends or go for dinner with his brother and his wife to retain a social life. Life was ok. It was nice.

Eric wasn't having an affair, he wasn't stealing from the company, he didn't drink and drive. He never even got a parking ticket. Eric paid his taxes and even tipped the bin men at Christmas with a twelve pack of premium beer, and not the little shitty French bottles that his neighbours gave away.

Eric Curtis was one of the ninety nine percent of law-abiding zombies who drift through life, following the path of least resistance and hoping for a few weeks in the sun once a year to have something to brag about on Facebook.

Eric's kids, Oscar and Kate, were successful at school and always said please and thank you to visitors if not always to their parents, and his wife, Jane, was still, in his eyes, the most beautiful woman he had ever been with and he loved her. He kept in reasonable – if not great - shape, running a few half-marathons a year and playing golf – and even had a full-on cliché of a mid-life crisis and bought a motorbike which he took out on one of the four weekends a year it wasn't raining.

Every day was the same, with just enough nuance to keep facing what Eric believed to be north and thinking he was staying fractionally ahead of everyone else who lived on his nice suburban street.

Eric would get up at 6:30 every morning from Monday to Friday, throw on a pair of jeans, button-down oxford shirt, glug down some coffee and bran flakes, make himself a packed lunch and then hit the M4, sticking the cruise control at fifty miles per hour through mile upon mile of untended and never-completed roadworks and arrive at the Harrow office at 8:30am like clockwork, parking in the space with the words "Eric Curtis, manager" stencilled onto the wall and sauntering into the office a full sixty seconds before his boss. Eric had made a career of getting promotions and bonuses by being at work before the guy who signs his cheques and staying until just after he's gone. The fact this made Eric's day a full two minutes longer than his boss's was incidental. Eric believed that what his manager didn't know wouldn't kill him (sadly) as there was quite a lot he didn't know. Eric always managed to use the sixty seconds he was in before his manager to make his desk look suitably messy and give the illusion he'd been in for hours. For all he knew, Eric had slept there. Eric didn't want his manager's job. He didn't even want his own, but it was better than being a plumber, or working in IT. Call centres. The coal mines of the twenty first century, but without the emphysema.

In Eric's experience, running a call centre was about as thrilling as it sounded. It consisted of reading reports, checking on his teams, lying to customers, fending off complaints from finance and HR about some made up report he had written but they couldn't understand. The highlight of his job were BV weeks. For the uninitiated, those are Boss Vacation weeks. When your boss is off you can pretend to be at an out-of-town conference and just actually work from home and grow roots on the couch watching Top Gear repeats.

Like clockwork at lunchtime, Eric would call Jane and ask how her day was going, not really listening to the answers and knowing she certainly didn't find his particularly inspiring either. After all, if Eric didn't, why would she? Eric would eat his home-made sandwich and packet of crisps and drink all the free coffee work supplied from a fluorescent-lit kitchen reserved for managers. The staff were blessed with an over-priced vending machine that sold chocolate bars and crisps, or a kebab van that was permanently parked outside, selling cardiovascular disease served in stale pitta bread. The Savoy Grill, it most certainly wasn't. Most would bring in their own lunch which was invariably a pot noodle or a tuna sandwich which added to the misery of the office by making it smell like a student's bedroom.

The boss would always leave at 5pm on the nose, and Eric would usually be heading for the M4 by 5:04pm. Eric had learnt to wait and watch for his boss's car to leave, as more than once Eric had run smack into him as he walked back into the building having forgotten something while he was legging it for the exit with his coat on. And that was never a good look.

And then to the unbridled joy of the journey home. More M4, more roadworks. More fifty miles per hour on cruise control, if he was lucky. Eric could do the journey and arrive at his house with no recollection of any part of it, such was the monotony he felt. Home for dinner, which was always chilli con carne on a Monday, chicken curry on a Tuesday, Spaghetti Bolognaise on a Wednesday, vegetable wraps on a Thursday and fish on a Friday. Saturday was takeaway night and always the same meal from the same Chinese restaurant, with a roast on a Sunday. Always either chicken or beef. Days blended into weeks, weeks blended into months and suddenly Eric Curtis was starting to go grey at the temples, looking forward to cups of tea and grunting when he sat down. A dumb hamster on a dumb wheel. It was awful and Eric could sense his life drifting away. He knew he was getting older and had a sense of time running out. He was in a rut and with every passing day it got deeper and deeper to the point where he could no longer see over the top.

The Curtis's had a dog. A Yorkshire Terrier they inherited from Eric's recently departed Mum. He was called Toto, Eric initially resented Toto but they had eventually learnt to co-exist and lately they were the only ones who even recognised the other's presence. He was old, toothless, stank of both bad breath and decay. He shook in terror when a goldfish broke wind next door, but yapped in furious anger when a Pitbull made the calamitous decision to sniff his arse in the park. He wasn't allowed on the couch, but Eric would often scoop him up and let him fall asleep on his lap while they lazed away those boring weekend afternoons.

And Eric drank. You wouldn't say he had a problem, but he liked a beer. No, he liked many beers. With dinner, after dinner and before bed. Never before 5pm except at weekends, where he'd start on the beers at lunchtime. It had got to the stage where Jane had stopped even mentioning it, and the kids would ask if he'd had a drink before asking him for help with their homework. Eric loved the buzz, the taste, and the way it helped him deal with the monotony of his life. He longed for some excitement.

Two

A word to the wise, though... be careful what you wish for.

This mundane existence that had taken root and was flourishing whether he liked it or not, changed a couple of months after his birthday. Jane had bought Eric another retro present which he'd relegated to the garage after a week: A camera. With film, and a tripod, and everything. Film. He wouldn't even know where to get film developed these days. Eric don't think Boots did it anymore, and when he sadly pointed this out to Jane, she went out and bought the developing kit and trays too. *'Awesome'*, thought Eric. *'More shit to bundle up and flog on eBay for a tenth of the price we'd paid* for it in three years' time'.

Of course, the first thing a man does when he gets a present like this is Google it to see what it's worth, just to check if his wife spent more than he did on her birthday present, which is never a good thing. Eric looked sadly at Jane's hardly-used exercise bike with bitter regret. What on earth was he thinking? They had 'enjoyed' a silent, angry Chinese takeaway that night, followed by six months of Eric telling her five times a day that he really didn't think she was fat at all.

Eric also had to Google all the instructions for the camera and dark room as he couldn't even switch the thing on without being shown what to do. He still don't know how men like him coped before YouTube.

So, in a typical bid to show willing, Eric would set off to the river, or to Oscar's football match, or to the local park with Toto, camera under his arm in the hope of snapping enough black and white arty pictures to prove he was taking this hobby seriously without expending any actual effort. That's a surprisingly easy balance to strike if you are committed to it. He'd get home, grab the trays and solutions and go into the cupboard under the stairs which in a rare display of impudence he'd converted into an improvised dark room and pretend to give a shit. Some of the pictures were alright. About as good as the ones he had already taken on his phone (which were coming in around £100 a print cheaper) but it kept Jane happy, and Eric busy, which is about as much as he could ask for. It was becoming obvious that hitting fifty meant Eric was no longer allowed to sprawl out on the couch from dawn till dusk on the weekend, drinking endless beers and eating crisps, thereby at a stroke banning the only activities he genuinely still loved to do.

This went on for a couple of weeks. There's a certain shelf-life to these things. A magical point in time at which you can slowly move the gift closer and closer to the shed, before you end up sneaking it in there when putting the bins out. It's never spoken of again. Jane's happy as she has some arty black and white prints of the kids that are framed and in the entrance hall, Eric is happy because Jane's happy that she thinks she got a clever present for him, and, most wondrously of all, he doesn't need to take the dog down to the river and take photos while following him around like some demented shit-slave, bagging his crap like a trophy while also stopping him from snarling at other dogs, and other people, and trees and air. So it's a win-win. Happy birthday. Next? How about a phone shaped like a hamburger, or a Reliant Robin?

While the camera nestled in its case, sitting at the back of the shed in between the creosote, rock-hard paint brushes and broken roof tiles, the collection of developing fluids and acetate acid sat, lurking and bubbling away on a bottom shelf like the cauldron from Macbeth. Eric had forgotten all about them. They'd probably still be there now if Oscar didn't want him to dig out his junior golf clubs that were sitting at the back of the shed under half tins of paint he kept "just in case", a broken bucket, a used-once Swingball and some more old tiles, this time from the roof of the last house they had lived in ten years earlier. Another man trait. They cannot bear to throw stuff out. More than once Eric had muttered to himself: 'If I cleared all this shit out I could squeeze an exercise bike in here'.

The Masters golf tournament at Augusta was on, and, like most kids, Oscar had wanted to replicate what was on the telly. So, as usual, he begged his dad to find his clubs so he could go into the garden and pretend to be Rory or Tiger for four days before losing interest as the last putt went in on the Sunday.

So, Eric dutifully dug the golf clubs out, knocking shelves and rusty tennis racquets and garden tools over as they snagged on everything within a five yard radius and smacked his head on the doorframe as he reversed out into the garden, swearing like a man who knows his kids are in earshot but also knowing it makes them laugh like drains. Jane tutted disapprovingly but she would swear like a Leeds United fan if Eric forget to record Love Island, so it was all good. Oscar scooped the clubs up and scarpered into the garden with some plastic balls and swiped away at them for an hour, digging trenches in the lawn and gradually knocking each one over the hedge and into next door's garden.

The golf finished at midnight, and Eric went to put Oscar's clubs away for their fifty one week hibernation.

As he did so, Eric opened the shed door to be met by an acrid smell of chemicals. He took what a junkie would call 'the full beans' down his throat and up his nose and almost immediately, everything started to go very, very foggy.

Three

Eric couldn't remember much about the next few days. He woke up in hospital the following Wednesday, surrounded by flowers from work, handmade cards from the kids (both beautiful and crap in equal measure and clearly created in minutes at their Mum's nagging insistence) and, most amusingly, a gas mask from his brother. Some very concerned looking doctors were milling around in the corridor outside Eric's ward, and he judged they were in earnest discussion about his plight. Eric was staring at them for only a few moments when one caught his eye and nervously prodded his colleagues. They all stopped at once and stared at their patient. Opened-mouth. 'Fuck', thought Eric. 'This can't be good'.

They refused to tell Eric anything until Jane arrived. 'Double fuck'. Eric was no expert, but he knew that if they were waiting for his next of kin to turn up then he probably wasn't getting the all-clear. They wouldn't even tell him what had happened. Eric had started to fill in those blanks himself. The fog in Eric's head was clearing a little. He remembered watching golf on TV. He could still practically taste the overcooked roast beef sandwiches and then his nose was filled with the sour smell of chemicals. Eric suddenly retched, managing to at least partially hit the little cardboard pot the nurses had kindly left on the table that covered his legs. Eric was never sure if he was supposed to pee or vomit in those things. Now he knew. The nurses appeared out of nowhere, fussing and tutting like he was a four year old who'd wet his bed.

Jane came in about an hour later, perched herself on the end of Eric's bed and opened her phone, scrolling through with typically detached boredom.

The doctor sat down, fixed Eric with a practiced smile and a dead-eyed stare that can only be taught at the 'how to tell a patient he's fucked' school and started talking.

"Eric. The thing is, you inhaled quite a lot of chemicals. Some of them had expired. Some of them were mixed when they really shouldn't have been, and they created a rather noxious substance. Some of them were ingested into your lungs and that's already permeated your brain. All of them are potentially fatal, or possibly harmless. We simply don't know what's likely to happen next. We're most terribly sorry".

Eric took this information surprisingly well, all things considered. He'd always been quite stoic about life, and simply swallowed hard, and with the exception of a single tear running down his cheek, he remained measured and calm. Jane sat, motionless, clutching her phone and gazing out of the window, obviously still relaxed from her massage.

"Am I dying?" Eric asked Jane, after the doctors had left. "Please tell me the truth"

"We're all dying" Jane replied, somewhat unhelpfully. "You're very pale though. Blood pressure is through the roof. They're worried about your heart rate and your brain function is apparently all over the place"

"Oh." he replied. And then she was off. She wanted to give her husband time to 'process' the information. Something she learned from Grey's Anatomy, probably. She said she had to make sure the kids were ok and had their tea.

Right. Time to find out how long he had left. Eric figured he should ask someone who at least had qualified at being an expert, rather than getting this information from YouTube.

"Well Eric, we think we know what you ingested. The problem is, no-one has been quite clumsy enough to consume as much as you did before and lived to tell the tale. We really don't know what will happen next. Technically, you should be dead and it's something of a happy mystery to us as to why you aren't. Any questions?".

"Well, yes", said Eric. "what are the chances I'll die from this?"

"I'm sorry, we don't know" replied the doctor.

"Will there be any psychological impact?" Eric asked

"We don't know" came the reply, "but everything *seems* normal so we're as sure as we can be that you'll be back to your old self in a few days".

Eric didn't like the emphasis on the word "seems" but decided to let it pass. "So I can go home?" he asked

"Oh yes, I think that would be ok. Stay here for one more night and we'll discharge you in the morning if nothing dramatic happens. Oh, and if you get home and notice any changes in your condition that worry you, pop back and see us and we'll get you in for a check-up".

"Changes?" queried Eric, "like what?"

"Oh, you know" replied the doctor. "If your blood pressure drops or you feel a bit odd, that kind of thing".

Eric has no idea what his blood pressure should be, or even how to measure it, so did what most people would do, and nodded in agreement and made a promise to keep in touch if he felt the need. Like most people, Eric hated being a nuisance and resolved to just take an aspirin and get back to work as soon as possible.

The next morning, Eric packed his cards, gas mask and clothes into a hospital-issued plastic bag and waited for the doctor to discharge him.

At exactly 11am, the doctor swept onto the ward. "Right Eric, everything looks fine. You're free to go. Remember, just pop back in here and see us if you think you need to, take it easy for a few weeks and I'd avoid drinking alcohol for a little while just to be on the safe side. All the best, cheerio". And, signing the discharge sheet with a flourish, he turned away and was gone.

Eric had already decided the first thing he'd do when he got home was open a beer, but he didn't think this worthy of mentioning so bade the departing doctor's back a hearty farewell, gathered his plastic bag and headed for the exit.

Eric got a taxi home. He'd called Jane but she hadn't answered, and all he wanted to do was get out of the hospital and away from the fluorescent lights and the incessant smell of disinfectant. He dumped his bag in the porch, grabbed his wallet and headed to the pub for a quick pint. It was his reward for cheating death, he thought to himself.

One pint turned into six, and by the time Eric staggered home the kids were in bed and Jane was off at her sister's house. 'Welcome home Eric', he thought glumly. Luckily, he had Toto waiting for him, sitting at the bottom of the stairs, angrily guarding a steaming pile of crap he'd made as some kind of delightful homecoming gift. It was more than anyone else had got for Eric, to be fair. He debated the age-old husband trick of ignoring it and pretending it had happened after he'd gone to bed, but in the hospital Eric had resolved to try and be a better father and husband so did the decent thing and bagged it up, cleaned the floor and dropped the crap surreptitiously into next door's recycling bin. 'Baby steps Eric, baby steps' he thought as he climbed into bed and immediately fell into a deep, dreamless sleep.

Four

The next few days were the start of the changes. Imperceptible at first, but looking back, they were there. While brushing his teeth, Eric noticed how pale he was when he looked in the mirror. Almost grey. If he had known what was to come, he would say translucent. Eric was struggling to eat solid food too. He hadn't eaten since having the roast beef sandwiches the night "it" happened and he was starving, but couldn't face more than some soup and coffee. Over the next few days Eric's appetite disappeared completely, and he started to struggle to fall asleep. Eric would close his eyes and still see bright lights. He couldn't face beer, and was always either too hot or too cold. Of all these symptoms, not being able to drink beer was the most alarming and he almost considered calling the hospital in a panic.

The kids were on school holidays, so they would go to the park, kick a ball around and throw sticks for (alright, at) Toto. He felt shit. Tired, lethargic but unable to sleep and Eric assumed it was just the after-effects of his "episode", as Jane had called it. Every day Eric thought about calling the doctor, but assumed that he'd be fine if he stopped complaining and got some rest. Eric figured his body was probably expelling the toxins of the chemicals he'd inhaled and would be fine in a week or so. Eric's boss was great - telling him to take a few weeks to recover. His brother asked for the gas mask back but didn't ask how Eric was feeling — simply telling Eric he needed it for a party he was going to, which was typical.

Eric woke the following morning to the unmistakable sound of an egg crashing against the bedroom window. He looked outside and saw the local gang of morons cackling and running away and a snotty yolk running down the glass. This happened once every few months and was about the most irritating thing about living in this town. Normally he would head out and chase them with a golf club, threatening to cut their balls off as they sprinted away in mocking glee, but even this wasn't enough to shake him from his stupor. Eric just shook his head, tutted and closed the curtains, he hoped to the gang's incandescent annoyance.

It was a full six days after what Eric alone had christened 'inhale-gate' that he started to really notice what was happening. He was brushing his teeth before bed and noticed the door reflected in the mirror behind him. He'd never seen it before from that angle, despite brushing his teeth in that sink twice a day for over twenty years. His brain tried to figure it out. How the fuck could he see the door while his body was blocking the mirror? He assumed he was seeing double and went to bed. Jane was unironically updating Facebook — pictures of the kids who she'd been screaming blue murder at for not going to bed on time five minutes earlier with '# the reason I breathe xx' and hardly noticed her husband climb in beside her. They muttered their goodnights and went to sleep. Twenty years of marriage? It takes more than a near-death experience to keep that fire burning brightly, obviously.

The next morning, she was gone. Off to work early. The kids were downstairs watching some idiotic shouty Instagram or YouTube channel where an eighteen-year-old millionaire was telling them how to shoot someone on an Xbox. Filled with bitter and resentful regret that he wasn't savvy enough to do that for a living, Eric went back upstairs to shower. Peeling his boxers and t-shirt off, he went to the bathroom and reached for the toothbrush. Eric Curtis couldn't see his hand.

Lots of things went through his mind at that moment, none of them rational:

"I'm dead. This is what death feels like"

"Jane didn't notice me last night. The kids didn't notice me this morning. I'm dead, and I'm a ghost. I'm in the sixth sense"

"This must be a dream. It's trippy as fuck man"

"Maybe I've gone blind?"

"Those pills I'm on must be making me hallucinate"

Eric did what any reasonable man on a sunny day off would do when faced with a moment of existential self-doubt. He assumed he was still dreaming and went back to bed.

He woke up a few hours later to the unmistakable sound of the kids calling him. It wasn't the usual panicky "Daaaaad" a parent gets when one of them has punched the other in the face, or "can we have chocolate?" (Default answer is either "ask your mother" or "yes" if she's not around). It was more an implied 'where the fuck are you Dad?'

Eric was lying on his bed. Bollock naked. Normally enough to have the kids run away in terror. Kate was in the room, looking right at him. "He's not here, fuckhead" she shouted at her brother.

Oscar stuck his head around the door. "He must have gone to the pub. I'm going to call him".

"He'll say yes anyway" said Kate, Let's just have half the chocolate each and hide the wrapper from mum. No point troubling him about it".

Eric lay in stunned silence as they raced downstairs. "What the actual fuck?" he thought to himself. He got up, went to the bedroom mirror. He must have stood there for a full three minutes. Agog, agape, aghast. Looking back at him was the unmistakable sight of the king-sized bed and ubiquitous studio photographic portrait of the family above the headboard. And nothing else. No shadow, no slightly greying but (in his mind) dazzling handsome Eric, no fuck-all. Jesus. he looked down. No hands, no arms, no feet, no six-pack (alright, that had disappeared thirty years ago), no shoulders, knees or toes, no old chap. Eric felt around. He could sense his arms moving, and that's when he started to wonder if he'd lost his mind.

Eric went downstairs in something of a trance. Still naked. He silently stood in front of the kids and blocked the shouty teenage millionaire they were so busy watching. Nothing. No screams of "get outta the way" or even "put some clothes on Dad, for fuck's sake". Nothing. Eric went to the kitchen, grabbed his phone and sent Kate a text. 'Gone to the pub, back in an hour'. He heard her phone beep. She told Oscar how she had been right, and then ensued a vigorous debate about who'd guessed Dad would be at the Red Lion. He could see the phone in his hand. He could see the keys being pressed. He could hear the floorboards gently creaking under his weight. He just couldn't see any part of him. At all.

Eric's brain kicked into overdrive. This wasn't a dream. He wasn't hallucinating. He was in-fucking-visible.

Eric took a selfie with his phone and checked the picture, and it was a lovely framed shot of the window behind him, looking into the garden. No sign of Eric. None. He was bad at taking selfies. His kids mocked him endlessly about cutting their heads off or "making them look ugly" but even he couldn't mess up a picture of himself from two feet away.

Eric started to think about what to do. Call the doctor? This surely ticked the 'anything unusual' box. He felt fine. Probably the best he'd felt since before sniffing chemicals. He sat down, gently closed the kitchen door and made himself a coffee.

It quickly became apparent to Eric that it was much harder doing stuff when a person can't see their hands than one might think. He nearly dropped the coffee tin, and the sugar. Co-ordinating hands you can't see took some getting used to but muscle memory kicked in and soon the smell of coffee filled his nostrils. He gulped down half the cup when a curious thought hit him. Eric shot back up the stairs, his cup appearing to float in front of him and drank some in front of the mirror. He could see the coffee in the reflection - right until it reached what he assumed was the bottom of his throat, at which point it vanished.

Then the doorbell rang. Eric went downstairs to see a delivery driver handing Kate a large parcel. He assumed it was probably some game-changing kitchen tool they didn't need and couldn't afford that Jane had bought from Amazon. Eric stood no more than three feet behind Kate. Naked, and hopefully invisible, or the courier would have at best run away screaming, or more likely called social services or the police. The fact he didn't even flinch despite Eric being almost close enough to touch gave him all the certainty he needed that he couldn't be seen.

Naturally, Eric was completely freaked out by this. His mind was screaming questions at him and he was already starting to join the dots about inhaling the photographic chemicals and his opaque colouring, but he still didn't make the leap that this was what had led to full transparency.

Eric, in a daze, stumbled back upstairs for a pee. That was barely visible too. He couldn't remember if that meant he was dehydrated or over hydrated. He guessed it probably didn't matter.

He washed his hands, noticing the hand shapes being created in the foaming soap, before they too disappeared under the running water. Wandering back into the bedroom He instinctively started to dress, putting his boxers and socks on. He went to open the wardrobe to grab a t-shirt when he noticed his reflection in the full length bedroom mirror - or, more accurately - the reflection of a floating pair of Marks and Spencer's finest cotton boxer shorts.

Eric thought no one saw him before, well now, they really wouldn't see him.

He had no choice. He needed answers.

He decided to call the hospital.

Five

Eric picked up the card the doctor had left him and dialled the number. "your call is important to us" came the inevitable reply from the automated greeting. "you are number forty three in the queue, and we'll answer your call as soon as possible".

Everyone has a skill they can call on when needed. A mechanic can replace his own fan belt, a plumber can unblock his own toilet, and Eric could tell straight away he was dialled into a call centre where he would be answered an hour later by someone who wouldn't be able to give him any useful advice or even transfer him to someone else who could. He noted sourly that the doctor hadn't given him his own direct number. No, that would be just silly. He'd given him the number of a company who answered calls on behalf of the hospital in a bid to save costs by never actually having to treat a patient in the flesh.

Eric knew he had to go back to the hospital, and quickly. His mind was scrambled but he was certain that being invisible was a state of affairs that needed professional attention, and quickly. Even in his panic Eric was sure that he shouldn't go wandering about the town naked, or even clothed but with a missing head. The less people knew about this the less panic he would create. And being English and reserved, he still didn't want to cause too much of a fuss. He knew he couldn't call a taxi and he soon realised driving himself was out of the question too. What would happen when he got out in the hospital car park and walked through reception? Then he remembered his motorbike. Eric dressed himself in jeans, boots, a jacket, gloves and put on his crash helmet and checked his reflection. He looked like a biker. And not an invisible one. Eric eased his motorbike out of the garage and rode the ten miles to the hospital. He dismounted, and keeping his helmet on, went inside.

The reception area was packed. Doctors and nurses milling about, patients sitting in the waiting area scrolling through their phones and a queue of people waiting to be checked in all added to the organised chaos. Eric decided against waiting at reception and headed back the general ward where he hoped he would find his doctor. Still wearing his biker gear and helmet, no-one gave him a second look.

After a ten minute walk through the maze of corridors, Eric found himself back on Ward F, and stood at the door looking in at the six occupied beds, each containing a patient, who were variously reading a paper or watching the rolling news channel on the one television that was bolted to the wall. None looked up as Eric turned and headed to the nurses station which was at the far end of the corridor.

There were no nurses. No doctors either. Just an empty desk with a dozen thank you cards from ex-patients and the families of those who's loved ones had been treated in this part of the hospital. Eric looked around for some assistance. He heard the sound of laughter from a door behind the nurses' station and pushed it open. Inside were three nurses, all laughing heartily as a DJ on the radio was telling a story about his weekend. Eric rapped on the door. The nurses turned as one, a look of resigned weariness replacing the smiles that were evident just moments earlier.

"Sorry love, we can't accept deliveries here, you need to go to reception" said the nurse in the dark blue uniform, who Eric guessed was the senior on duty.

"I need to see a doctor" replied Eric. "I think it is quite urgent".

The nurse looked puzzled. "Sorry my darling, I can't hear a word with that helmet on. Visiting hours are three to five, and seven till nine. Can you come back then?"

Eric opened his visor a little so his voice would be less muffled. "I. Need. To. See. A. Doctor" he said. As clearly, loudly and confidently as he could.

"Yes, in that case, head back to reception and they'll send you to Accident and Emergency. We can't help you here".

The nurse clearly wanted Eric to go to reception, and realising this conversation was going nowhere, he turned and left. As he departed, he could hear more laughter from the office and assumed that this was aimed at him and his inability to go to reception when repeatedly asked.

Eric headed back towards the main building and had an idea. He slipped into an unoccupied changing cubicle and undressed. He folded his clothes neatly into a pile, carefully balancing his crash helmet on top and walked back towards the laughing nurses. Fully naked, he padded his way down the maze of corridors, pausing to peer into various open doors in the hope of finding his doctor. He finally arrived back on his ward and saw a gaggle of nurses around a bed, and — hallelujah! — his original doctor in the middle of the group doing his rounds.

Nurses were hanging on his every word, scribbling instructions and nodding at every word he uttered. Eric watched as they bustled from bed to bed. The patients were barely being acknowledged and certainly not being asked for their opinions, such was the speed the doctor moved. He completed each ward of six beds in less than six minutes, and Eric stood in silent awe at his confidence and pace as years of experience flowed from him. A fleeting thought crossed his mind that patient care seemed secondary to the need to see every patient in as short a timeframe as possible and Eric considered how he would grab his doctor's attention. Until this point, he hadn't even thought was he was going to say. The outline of his plan was to simply reveal himself and hope the doctor would immediately recognise Eric and his symptoms and provide an immediate solution.

Eric positioned himself at the end of corridor and waited for the doctor to finish his rounds. Soon enough he did, and bade the nurses a pleasant afternoon and headed towards Eric. As he steamed purposefully down the hall, his phone rang. Muttering an angry "for fuck's sake, what now?" he answered. "Dr Rice, what is it?" Eric steeled himself for the impending collision.

Doctor Rice brushed Eric aside as if he weren't there. Eric put a meek hand out to halt the doctor's progress but it hardly registered. The doctor didn't break stride but instead started giving instructions to his caller about medicinal dosages and 'plenty of fluids'. As Doctor Rice reached the double doors that led him back into the main body of the hospital he paused and turned, seemingly unsure of feeling something. He shook his head, pushed through the doors and was gone. Eric chased after him. He knew he had to get help and he didn't know who else he could talk to. As Eric threw open the doors he was greeted with the sight of the busy reception area and absolutely no sign of Doctor Rice. It was as if he had simply vanished. The irony of this was not lost on Eric.

Eric went back through the doors and back to his changing cubicle. He dressed in his motorcycle gear, put his helmet back on and headed back to the car park. He was angry, confused, frightened and just wanted to get the hell out of there.

What he hadn't seen was one particular patient. A man in his forties, smartly dressed in a suit, sitting quietly in one corner of the waiting area. Not reading a newspaper, not watching the TV, and not scrolling through his phone, but rather studiously watching the other patients come and go, watching nurses and doctors scurrying around, and watching doors be flung open with no-one walking through them. And he found that to be very interesting. Very interesting indeed.

Eric jumped back on his bike. Revved the engine and sped out of the car park. Behind him, peering out of a dirty third floor window, the man in the suit from the waiting room silently watched Eric leave.

Six

As he arrived home he gently nursed the bike back into the garage, undressed, and headed to the pub. Eric decided he needed time to process all this and the Red Lion was going to have to be a place to sit and think. He had lost his taste for beer but resolutely decided to smash through that symptom and cure himself of this particular malady. It was now after lunchtime, and the bar would certainly be pretty empty and he always did his best thinking in the pub.

Eric had never walked out of his house naked (when not in a dream, anyway), and he found it both alarming and wonderful at the same time. Knowing no-one could see him would have been life-affirming, but he still wasn't totally convinced. It was only when he arrived at the pub that he really started to think he was in the clear. He'd walked past a couple who were out shopping, and a few cars had driven past. No-one had cried out in fright or honked their horns - not even a second glance in his direction. "I am rocking this", thought Eric, for the first time feeling slightly in control. Carefully dodging piles of dog shit and broken glass, he strode the five hundred metres to The Red Lion, pushed the door open and walked in.

At this point, two things happened. First, the barmaid looked up in alarm at her door swinging open. Eric gulped - then she went back to her Sudoku while a panel show of men-hating housewives screeched angrily on the TV in background. Eric breathed a large sigh of relief. Until the second thing happened. The pub's Alsatian went absolutely mad. It went bat shit crazy. Eric had seen dogs lose their shit before. Usually aimed at Toto who did manage to bring out the angry in most living things - but this was off the scale. He came running towards Eric, all teeth and snarls and he only just managed to jump up onto a table before the dog snipped his bollocks off with his teeth.

The barmaid shot round to the table Eric was standing on and tried to grab the dog by the collar. He paced up and down, round the table - as confused as any dog has been before. Finally, the barmaid was able to shepherd the Alsatian into the room behind the bar and Eric breathed a sigh of relief. Eric knew the dog could clearly sense him — he wasn't sure if he could smell him, but had to assume he could. Had Eric actually shat himself instead of only metaphorically doing it then he might have found out. Once the dog was out of the bar Eric settled down and decided on his next move. By now he was gasping for a beer but it was dawning on him that it would be hard - being invisible and all - to stroll up to the barmaid and ask for a pint. Also, given his state of undress he had forgotten to bring his wallet and although Eric could probably have claimed a free one as a result of being something of a novelty decided this might be a risky move. He made the ultimately brave and heroic call of legging it with a lesson learnt. Dogs are potentially going to blow his cover.

Eric headed outside and almost walked straight into the gang who'd egged his house just days earlier. They were all swagger and bravado, talking in New York street slang and calling each other 'bruv' and talking about 'da bitches' of Berkshire. William Wordsworth, they weren't. A fleeting thought of swinging a punch or two crossed his mind but he quickly brushed it away. This would probably end badly and the fun would be over before it started. So, Eric pinned himself to the wall of the pub and let them saunter past. He watched them go with glowering contempt and a wish that he was a slightly braver, stronger man and not terrified of teenagers.

Eric wandered up the high street and into the newsagent that doubled as an off licence. The door was propped open. No problems there. No dogs trying to kill him. Good. He walked quietly to the fridge. The shopkeeper was busy reading his newspaper. The shop was empty. He didn't look up. Also good. Eric slid the fridge door open and picked up a can of lager. Instinctively, and rather than doing the smart thing of waiting until he was out of earshot, He popped the ring pull thinking he could down a beer while the shopkeeper was reading about how the latest stabbing was hurting house prices in the town. And here's another lesson; Eric might be invisible, but he is not close to being silent. Things he does make a noise as normal. And shopkeepers who own off licences can hear an illegal ring pull from 80 paces. Shit.

The next minute or so was something of a blur, but it went something like this. Click, Fsshhhhhhh. "WHAT THE FUCK???". Then the sound of a can dropping, Eric's feet smacking hard against the shop floor and a break for freedom. He bravely legged it. He only stopped running about three hundred yards up the road when it was obvious he wasn't being chased. Eric jogged back towards the off-licence (on the other side of the road, of course) and stared through the window. To his amazement, the shopkeeper was back, leaning against the counter, reading his paper.

Eric tiptoed into the shop. He couldn't see his beer - so tried to figure out what on earth had happened when another customer came in. He walked straight to the beer fridge and grabbed a six pack. The shopkeeper looked up.

"Careful mate - I'd grab some bottles if I were you. Once of those cans just blew. Might be a dodgy batch, I'll be sending them back this week". The customer carefully dropped the cans he was holding back on the shelf like they were an armed bomb, and picked up some bottles and went to pay. Eric breathed a huge sigh of relief. While the customer and shopkeeper were engaged in some idle conversation, he snuck out and headed home, just as it started to rain heavily. Luckily, no pedestrians were there to see the footprints he was making, and he got home, cold, wet, but unscathed.

Eric knew he'd have to tell Jane. It was inconceivable that he could carry this on without her. He was sure she would begin to notice that her husband was invisible eventually. Granted, given the state of their relationship it could take a couple of weeks, but in that moment Eric needed her. She was the one person who knew him better than anyone, and despite the obvious boredom they felt in their marriage he always loved hearing his wife's opinions. She had always been the sensible one, making sure she remembered their friends' birthdays, paying the bills on time and saying no when he wanted permission to buy a sports car with his own money. He knew she would – once she had a chance to hear from him what had happened – take a pragmatic view on what to do.

Eric sent her a text she'd sent him numerous times. The one that makes every husband or boyfriend's heart stop.

'We need to talk'

Seven

Eric had this text sent to him several times during the course of their marriage. Eric used to think, mostly, this was to test him and try and judge his reaction. Given he'd never cheated he used to assume she'd found his internet browser history (which would be bad), a forgotten wank sock under the bed (worse) or opened messages on his phone where he had flirty drunken messages from her sister, received last Christmas, and safely archived for 'personal use' (unquestionably catastrophic). In every case it was something far more trivial. A child had received a poor school report, or Toto had crapped in the laundry cupboard. Always Eric's fault, of course. After all, he had only locked him in there once, and that was because he'd bared his teeth at Eric after being told off for taking a dump in Eric's favourite slipper.

Jane replied straight away. She sounded properly rattled.

*"What's the matter? Is it the kids? Are you ok? Tell me". S*he texted

Eric replied that it was nothing they could discuss over the phone, and to get home as soon as she could. He was relieved to see the kids had gone out. They'd helpfully left a note.

'Took £20 from your wallet, have gone out. Back later. Dog has had a dump in the kitchen'. Eric's shoulders slumped.

Twenty minutes later, Jane appeared. Eric was waiting in the kitchen when she rushed in. When he saw that look of panic on her face he was immediately in love again. She looked vulnerable, worried and beautiful all at once and it made him remember the many things that he'd found so attractive all those years ago. They had met just as she was escaping from an abusive relationship. She worked for him in some god forsaken administration office where Eric was a young, up and coming management trainee, and he had started to notice she was in early and going home late, and was wearing make up to hide bruises.

Eric had helped her find a new flat and given Jane an advance on her salary to pay the deposit, and then changed her shift patterns so her ex-boyfriend never knew when she would be in the office. He hadn't wanted a relationship in return, this was just Eric's nature. But Jane had invited him to dinner a few weeks after moving into her new apartment, and Eric stayed the night and they'd been together ever since. Jane now worked as a counsellor, helping abused women at a shelter, and despite an obvious lack of funding had helped countless people escape some horrible situations.

Jane stood in the middle of the kitchen and called Eric's name. Eric sidled up behind her and whispered "hello Jane". Spinning round, she stared right through her husband. She called out again.

Eric spoke softly. "Jane, I'm here. I'm right in front of you", and he gently took her hand.

Looking back, this was a mistake. It would have been easier to have written a note, or sent a text, or even recorded a video and emailed it to her. Clutching someone's hand when they can't see who is touching them, or aren't expecting it, in a room full of both sharp and blunt objects in equal measure, could be extremely hazardous to someone's health. Jane screamed, recoiled and grabbed a frying pan all in one swift, poetic movement. That it was full of greasy water ('soaking in the sink' - a euphemism for 'can't be fucking arsed to wash it now') probably saved Eric's life. It was heavier than she'd expected and she was slower bringing it towards his head than she would have otherwise been. Instinctively, Eric let go of her hand and stepped backwards. His naked foot landing squarely in the pile of Toto's crap.

Repulsed, Eric yelled at the top of his voice "Christ Toto, you little BASTARD". That seemed to break Jane's spell. She dropped the pan and stood, open mouthed, her eyes darting between where the voice was coming from and the levitating dog shit which was smeared under Eric's foot as he hopped towards the counter that housed the roll of paper kitchen towels.

"Eric?" It was definitely a question. "What the actual fuck". That wasn't.

Wiping away the last of Toto's semi-digested breakfast, Eric quickly washed his hands and approached Jane again. "Jane, it's me. Don't freak out. I need you to stay calm. I'm freaking out myself. I need your help. Please help me". She could hear the very, very real panic in Eric's voice. "Come and sit down in the living room" he said. "I'll try and explain"

Eric followed her to the living room. Her mouth was wide open and her eyes searching for how this trick was being done, but she was in deep shock and not screaming in terror, so he felt assured he could work with that. She sat on the sofa, and Eric sat on the footstool opposite her, no more than twelve inches away. Eric initially thought this was because he wanted to give her reassurance, but it was probably subconsciously because any punches she landed from that distance would be less likely to hurt as she hadn't had a proper run up.

Eric took a deep breath, and began: "Jane, listen. I don't know what's happened. For the last few days I've been getting paler and paler, I think it was those chemicals I inhaled"

"Ingested" she said. "You ingested them". Always a stickler for factual accuracy, was Jane.

Eric stopped himself from sighing. Now was not the time to pick a fight. He replied, "Whatever. But this morning I'm gone. I'm here, but I'm gone, you can touch me, and I can touch stuff, but, as you can see, well as you can't see, I'm invisible.". He took hold of her hand, preventing her recoil, and placed it on his face. She touched Eric's cheek, moved her hands over his neck, and his arms and then down to his chest.

"You're naked!" She exclaimed. "You're wandering around the house, naked" Also, not a question.

And so it began. An hour or more of questions (or not), talking, tears, panic and then the dawn of understanding. She really had taken it better than Eric. As a trained counsellor Jane was an expert in listening, probing and being non-judgmental. He explained about his trip to the hospital and his need for answers and the way his request for help had been brushed off. He told Jane about his trip to the pub and the dog that wanted his testicles for a trophy, and his visit to the newsagent. They started to speak about what they should do or who they should call when the front door slammed both open and then shut in one poetic movement. A skill only a fourteen-year-old girl can truly master. Kate marched up the stairs without stopping to give Jane a second glance. Admirably, Jane then remembered they had kids. "And what do we tell them?" she asked quietly, nodding over her shoulder. Definitely a question.

They decided not to tell them. At least not yet. What Eric loved most about Jane was her ability to see the practicalities during adversity. Crashing her car was the chance to upgrade and screw the insurance company. Bad weather meant she had to buy a new coat. That kind of thing. Jane's advice kept returning to calling the doctor, but when Eric gave her the phone number she dialled it and gave up when she heard the automated message that she was number sixty-three in the queue. Jane suggested they both go to the hospital, but now it was getting late and they decided Doctor Rice would be off home and the can of worms this would open would end up with one, or both of them being committed to a secure facility somewhere. Jane had some contacts in the health service through her work but couldn't find one who could offer practical help in this situation.

"So you didn't go into the bank today and steal a few quid?" She asked later when the kids were tucked up and asleep. "That's what I'd have done. God knows the shelter could do with the funding". Eric asked her where he should have rolled up and stuck the money he'd nicked, given a wad of cash seemingly floating down the street would look a little odd and probably lead to him being chased by everyone who saw it. They both laughed at the obvious connotation of her husband shoving a grands worth of tenners up his arse. It was the first time they had laughed in each other's company in a year.

By this time, Eric had started to come to terms with this situation and had begun to see the potential financial opportunities that this predicament could be offering. There wasn't an obvious solution unless they could convince Doctor Rice to take them seriously, which seemed unlikely. They didn't know who else to talk to and besides, Eric wasn't in any pain and in all probability any doctor who did take him seriously wouldn't be able to do much except call the authorities and have him sent off to a lab somewhere for analysis. Eric hated his job and would have done anything to keep paying the mortgage without having to submit to the M4 twice a day. Notwithstanding the fact that this affliction could go as quickly as it came, it did present some obvious logistical challenges.

Why couldn't they steal a few quid and pay the mortgage? Why couldn't they use the cash to get the kids a couple of nice gifts? They hadn't had a holiday in years and while they could pay the bills, there was never enough left over for luxuries. And surely the shelter Jane worked at could use some extra funding, if no-one got hurt obtaining it? That final point felt justification enough to at least talk about how they could do something constructive with Eric's invisibility.

The Curtis's semi-nefarious plan would involve no-one knowing about Eric's condition and there wasn't a chance in hell their kids wouldn't be bragging about this to their mates at school. One of Oscar's friend's dad was a pilot. A fact he mentions whenever he would visit for dinner. Eric being invisible would give Oscar the chance of one-upmanship that Oscar could never pass up, and should the world get to hear there was an invisible man on the loose then society may take a different approach to their security, and Eric would be locked up for experiments for the rest of his life. Well, that's what they told themselves, anyway.

Eight

Eric woke with a start. It was mid-morning and Jane was gone. The kids were gone. He started to panic. He needed Jane. Before he went into a meltdown she breezily appeared, holding a mug of steaming coffee and a bacon sandwich. Eric was starving, and realised he hadn't really eaten in days. Jane watched him closely, noticing the food disappear as it reached his gullet.

"What's the plan, Stan?" She asked, smilingly. "What are we doing first? Robbing a bank or stealing a car?". She'd clearly been giving this a lot of thought. "Eric, what I do really matters. It changes people's lives in way you can't imagine. If we can find a way to inject some cash into the shelter it would mean we could save some women who are in real danger from further abuse".

Eric thought about this for a while. He knew Jane's work was important and he loved her for doing it. He wanted to make her happy, and he wanted to do the right thing but he also knew he couldn't possibly return to work like this and they had to pay the bills somehow. He suggested a compromise.

"Why can't we do both?" he asked. "A few quid for us, and a few quid for the shelter? Just to cover the bills and help a few of your more deserving cases".

Jane saw the conundrum. Her salary wouldn't be enough to keep them afloat and if he was carted off by the health professionals, she didn't think they'd be able to cope. She agreed.

Eric showered and put on a dressing gown, and they went downstairs to begin to plan their next moves.

"Umm, where are the kids?" asked Eric. He generally wouldn't have noticed their absence but the TV was off and the house was eerily quiet.

"I've shipped them off to my sisters for a few days" she explained. "I told them you were going through something of a breakdown and needed space". Although that was probably closer to the truth than Eric cared to admit, he did wonder aloud if Oscar and Kate would understand when they inevitably discovered the truth. Eric believed that breakdowns were things only cars had, and the stigma attached to "not being well" as his Mum would call it meant he was somehow less of a man.

Jane said "it's the 2020s now, and the kids will be just fine so stop worrying. They know you have been under pressure and it's perfectly normal to seek help". Eric wasn't convinced, but knew his wife was well trained in these things so accepted her point of view and pushed the thoughts from his mind.

They sat at the dining room table. Jane pulled out a pad and a pen and wrote "WAYS TO STEAL MONEY" in big letters at the top. Jane loved a list. They were everywhere. Shopping lists, birthday lists, lists about lists. She couldn't help herself. Nothing in life couldn't be made simpler without one of Jane's lists. She sucked on the end of her biro and looked at her words. "We probably shouldn't be writing this down, should we?" she asked with a resigned sigh. "Christ, twenty seconds in and we're already amassing evidence. I might as well email this to the police". She crumpled up the paper, found a box of matches and took it into the garden. Jane poured lighter fluid over it and dropped the match. Naturally it didn't catch fire, but a gust of wind whipped the paper from her hand and she spent the next few minutes chasing it round the garden until she finally pounced on it. She crumpled it up even more and proceeded to begin to tear it into tiny pieces before popping it into her mouth.

Eric watched this unfold while leaning against the back door with a huge grin on his face. "Would you look at us" he said. "I don't think Columbo would be shitting himself when it comes to cracking this case, do you?". Jane tried to gulp down the last of the paper, only for Eric to remind her it was doused in lighter fluid. This caused her to retch noisily. Eric gathered up the soggy remnants of the list and flushed them, strip by strip down the toilet.

They headed back to the dining room table. Eric took the pen and blank pad of paper and shoved them into the kitchen drawer.

Eric began. "Ok, so If we're going to steal anything we must make sure no-one gets scared, and no-one gets hurt. We only steal what we need, and we only steal from people who can afford it, agreed?"

Jane nodded. "How about robbing a bank?" She asked. "Sneak into a vault, stay there the night and creep out in the morning past any bank staff".

"Where do you suggest I carry the money?" Eric replied. "It's not going up my arse, remember?"

Jane suggested "Why don't you leave it somewhere and I'll pick it up in the morning?".

"I think they'd spot a pile of money hidden behind a plant pot, don't you?" said Eric. Jane visibly baulked at the rebuke and Eric immediately apologised. "Sorry darling, there is no such thing as a bad idea, ok?"

"Ok, thank you" said Jane

"Except that one. That was just awful" laughed Eric and the tension lifted.

"What about stealing a car?" asked Jane

"I thought of that" replied Eric, "and it would be fun, but do you know anyone who buys stolen cars? Where would we sell them, and I think we'd need to steal a lot to make it worthwhile".

Jane agreed they didn't know anyone who would buy stolen cars.

"How about doing some insider trading?" Jane asked. "You could sneak into a board meeting at your company and see if you could get information that we could use to beat the stock market".

Eric thought for a moment. "Well, not only do I know less than fuck all about the manipulation of a share price, but I don't even know where we'd go to buy or sell any shares in the first place".

Eric spoke next. "How about we work as a team to steal money from shops? You could walk into a shop, distract the shopkeeper while I hop behind the counter and rifle through the till. I'd stash the cash somewhere near the door and you could go and collect it once the shopkeeper is serving someone else".

Sitting at the kitchen table, this plan made perfect sense. It seemed beyond foolproof. Eric disrobed, and they set off the mile or so to the local High Street.

Nine

The first shop they came to was a charity shop. Jane went to go in and Eric gently steered her away. They may have been wannabe petty criminals but stealing from a shop which provided financial help to cancer sufferers felt a step too far. Eric pointed out that stealing from a charity to give to another charity didn't seem like they were truly sticking it to the man as they'd promised each other.

So, they pressed on and arrived at the local hardware store. Eric whispered in Jane's ear that he could hide any stolen money in one of the buckets that was for sale and piled up in neat columns near the door. He'd simply drop another bucket on top, hiding the money from view, and Jane would buy the top two buckets and scurry home with them. Jane started to point out that they didn't need any buckets but stopped herself when she realised that wasn't really the point.

The shop was empty except for Mr King, the owner, who stood inside on a small stool while he refilled a head-high shelf with boxes of screws and nails. As the Curtises entered, he turned and gave Jane a cheery wave and bade her good morning. Eric felt a pang of shame. Was this really the right thing to be doing, stealing from an elderly man in a long brown coat who sold nails for a living? Then he saw that he was charging a tenner to have a key cut and immediately changed his mind. "I'm Robin Hood, stealing from the rich to give to the needy. And my bank manager is very needy", he thought to himself. Eric thought of the women in Jane's shelter and metaphorically slapped himself. This wasn't about him, it was about her and her life's work. This may have been only a partial truth, but he felt emboldened by it and pressed on.

Jane walked past the shopkeeper and spent a few minutes nervously looking around the store as if she were lost. Eric watched Mr King as his eyes followed her every movement with careful concentration so he didn't fall off his stool. He clearly didn't trust anyone and eyed her suspiciously. Eventually he stepped off his stool and approached Jane.

"Help you miss?" he asked kindly. Eric felt another pang of shame for being so judgmental. Here was an old man in his own store and he had only been watching Jane to make sure she was ok. Eric pushed the thought aside. This was a trial run. They'd return any money they stole and use the experience to take on a megastore who were more deserving targets for their heinous crimes.

Jane smiled and said "I need a...". She looked nervously around the store for something out of sight that she might need. "a....chainsaw. Do you sell them?". A chainsaw. Eric groaned silently to himself. This was a small independent hardware store. They sold nails, paint, superglue, that type of thing. There was no chance on God's earth Mr King would sell a chainsaw. Why would Jane ask for a fucking chainsaw. Of all the things...Eric's furious internal monologue was interrupted by Mr King's reply:

"Why yes of course, I have a couple of those over in the far corner, let me show you. Follow me dear" and with that he led her away and left Eric standing by the till, all alone.

Eric took his chance while the shopkeeper was distracted. He nipped behind the counter, pushing the 'no sale' button on the cash register. He tensed, expecting a bell to ring or an alert to go off, but it just slid effortlessly open and there, sitting in front of him, was a stack of ten and twenty pound notes.

Eric looked over at Jane who had noticed the till was open and she immediately stepped sideways so her body was blocking Mr King's view of the counter. She had picked up a chainsaw and was trying to think of an intelligent question to ask about it when

Eric scooped up a pile of notes and walked back to the door, dropping what he guessed was a hundred and fifty pounds in a bucket before silently placing another bucket on top so the cash was hidden from view. Eric then slipped out of the shop and headed home to wait for Jane and their ill-gotten gains.

Jane appeared at home ten minutes later, carrying two buckets as agreed. She handed them over with a triumphant flourish and Eric prized them apart. They were both conspicuously empty.

"Ummm. Right. I'm sure I dropped a wad in cash into the top bucket, then placed another one on top of it. The money was there" Eric began.

"Oh God, I'm sorry" replied Jane. "Maybe it fell out? I'll walk back into town and see if it's lying around"

"It couldn't have fallen out" suggested Eric. "And anyway, if it did the wind would have carried it far away by now. Are you sure you picked up the buckets by the door?"

"No. You said the buckets by the till!" exclaimed Jane. Eric assured her that no, it was the buckets by the door although in the excitement admitted that he now couldn't actually remember which bucket he'd agreed to drop the money into.

"Perhaps I can go back and exchange these buckets for the ones by the door" proffered Jane.

"Yeah, that wouldn't be weird at all" replied Eric. "They're all the same colour but you want to exchange two buckets for two identical buckets because...?"

"I've got it, I'll just go and buy the other buckets" said Jane excitedly.

"So let me get this straight. You went into a hardware store to buy a chainsaw, but instead walked out with two buckets, which in itself it an unusual purchase. And now you want to go back in and buy two more buckets and you don't think that will look a little odd? How many buckets do you think the average person needs?". Eric's question was clearly rhetorical, and Jane admitted she'd not only never bought a bucket before but couldn't imagine a scenario where more than one was required, let alone four.

It was obvious to them both that they were a bit shit at this. Rather than go back to the store and buy more buckets and try and convince Mr King that they were just starting a collection of buckets, they agreed that discretion was the better part of valour and they'd be better off forgetting the whole thing.

Stealing from shops seemed fraught with difficulties and felt like a lot of risk for not much reward.

Ten

The industrial estate-style shopping centre on the far side of town was populated with the usual collection of DIY superstores, sofa warehouses and fast food outlets. It also had a large self-storage facility where people locked up their unused possessions and paid a monthly fee to keep them safe. Eric had used one to house his Mum's furniture after she'd died a few years previously. He had bought a padlock, hired a van and dumped seventy years of unwanted belongings in a corner unit for three months before using some of the inheritance he'd been given to pay someone to go and take almost all of it to the local tip.

"Why don't we go and explore some of the lock-ups and see if there are any hidden treasures stashed away in those?" Eric had suggested.

It seemed like the most workable plan they had come up with, so Jane headed back to the DIY shop, bought a pair of bolt cutters and rented a small unit in the storage facility to hide them on site. They went into the reception area, paid the deposit and advance monthly fee while Eric sat unnoticed in reception. The member of staff helped Jane complete the forms to reserve unit number six and showed her where it was. Jane took a single cardboard box containing the hidden bolt cutters and placed it carefully before securing the door with the combination lock, promising the girl behind the counter she'd be back in a few days with the rest of the boxes she was planning to store there.

Jane left just as the storage depot was closing for the night, and Eric got up, stood behind the receptionist and watched as she punched in the security codes for the gates and alarm system, before grabbing her coat and leaving for the night as the shutters closed behind her. Eric was alone in a dark, cold warehouse. The green fire exit lights were giving off an eerie green glow and he waited for thirty minutes to be sure the coast was clear.

Eric tiptoed over to the alarm as slowly as he could and entered the number into the keypad. The door remained closed but the light on the panel turned from red to green. Next, he typed in the code for the CCTV system and it unlocked the monitor. The screen flickered into life and he could see twenty four small screens, all showing different views of the building from both the inside and outside. Eric reached around the back and pulled the power cord from the CPU and the screen immediately went black. He hoped this meant the cameras wouldn't be recording. He had a similar CCTV system in his call centre from which he could watch as his staff took surreptitious cigarette breaks and knew that it was very unlikely the system would be being backed up if the power went off.

Finding the door to unit number six was easy, but seeing the numbers on the combination lock was much harder. The limited light forced Eric to hold the lock inches from his face while he twisted and fiddled with the keys, before finally and mercifully he heard the click as it opened. He felt his way inside the small container and used his foot to find the box in the dark. He pulled it open and retrieved a shiny set of bolt cutters and headed back into the corridor.

Eric wasn't really sure what he was looking for, but guessed he would have a nosey around and if there was anything valuable he could simply move it into his own storage unit and have Jane retrieve it when the coast was clear.

He decided to open a handful of doors at random. If number 6 was the only lock unbroken it wouldn't be difficult to conclude that was suspicious.

'lucky number seven', thought Eric. He gripped the ends of the cutter and snapped the lock off in a single snip. He picked up the broken lock and dropped it into the bolt cutter box that he had carried with him, and stepped inside. Pitch black. 'Oh for fuck's sake' he hissed angrily. He couldn't see a thing inside the unit. Cursing his stupidity that he hadn't asked Jane to pack a torch, he headed out and back to reception, rifling through cupboards and drawers in desperation. In the last drawer he searched he found a cigarette lighter. Not perfect, but it would have to do. He flicked the lever a couple of times and it gave off a small but useful flame.

Eric headed back to unit seven, turned on the lighter and peered inside. He could just make out a pile of boxes so walked over to them and pulled the top one open. The lighter was getting hot and burning his fingers, so he used it as sparingly as he could. He flicked the lighter again and could make out a pile of old clothes. Closing the box, he felt his way to open the second and third boxes, which yielded the same paltry treasure. He counted a dozen boxes and rather than wasting more time sifting through someone's old wardrobe moved on to unit number twelve.

Unit twelve was locked, but the padlock came off as easily as the first one and in he went, using the lighter to check inside. Engine parts and a set of spare wheels stared silently back at him. Another bust.

He headed further down the corridor to unit twenty. Eric broke in, dropping the lock into his box and inspected the contents. A small wooden crate sat in the corner. Prising the lid open he peered inside. It was full of bags of white powder. Eric had never even seen drugs before. He immediately closed the lid. It could have been cocaine or flour for all he knew, and would know anyone who could tell the difference. He knew that whatever it was, and however much it's street value, he and Jane wouldn't have a clue what to do with it. He moved on.

Eric made his way to the stairwell, and found the steps leading up to the second of four floors. Unit number thirty two met him as he pushed open the door and he made his way inside. More boxes of clothes. Units forty and forty eight contained old furniture and when he reached the third floor he was starting to give up hope. Eric reached unit number sixty and popped the lock open.

Inside was a toolbox and shelving, neatly laid out with tools, screws, nails and mercifully, a torch. His fingers were now painful with the heat from the lighter and he gratefully grabbed it, pushing the button and smiling in relief as the light filled the container. Finally, Eric's luck had changed. This was about to get a whole lot easier. Eric stepped out of the unit and into the corridor, moving the torch from side to side to find another door. That's when he looked through the window and into the car park and saw a policeman, standing outside and looking up at the single bright torchlight flashing back at him from an otherwise darkened building.

'Ah crap' said Eric out loud, turning the torch off and dropping it. The policeman was still looking up, but was by now speaking into his radio. Eric managed to find the torch and scooped it up, along with the box of broken locks and he ran back to unit six as fast as he could. He stashed the box and the torch in the corner, and locked the unit before heading to reception.

The policeman was standing outside, peering through the glass into the darkness of the reception area. Eric fumbled for the power cable to the CCTV and plugged it back in, causing the screens to blink into life. He walked to the front door and waited, knowing that back up would soon be arriving and his best chance of getting away was to sneak through the door as soon as it was opened.

Twenty minutes later the girl who had helped Jane earlier that evening arrived with a set of keys and let the policeman in. She punched in the alarm code. "that's odd, I am sure I set it earlier" she said.

"Stay here ma'am" the policeman instructed. "check the CCTV and shout if you see anything suspicious. I'll take a look around". By now, Eric was running across the car park and towards the main road. Jane had agreed to pick him up at 8am when the centre opened, and had gone home for the night. With no phone Eric had no option but to walk home and hope to God he wouldn't be implicated in the break in.

Eric arrived home just after midnight. Jane was naturally surprised to see him.

"Have the police been here?" panted Eric, brushing stones from the soles of his feet.

"No, why? What happened?" asked Jane who was starting to panic.

Eric filled Jane in on the events of the evening. The police hadn't been round. The husband and wife tried to work out if the police held Eric's fingerprints on file and agreed that they had been stupid not to wear gloves. Eric couldn't remember ever being fingerprinted in his life, so assumed he wouldn't be implicated, but he still googled the local news websites and checked social media. There were no reports of any mysterious break-ins at the self-storage and they went to bed with Jane suggesting it was time to head back to the purely metaphorical drawing board.

Eleven

Eric and Jane spent many hours trying to work out how to make their situation profitable.

"How about breaking into houses at night and seeing what cash was lying about?" asked Eric

"We only take from people who deserve it or who can afford it, remember?" replied Jane. "And anyway, people hardly use cash these days and it feels a bit high risk and enormous effort for potentially bugger all in return".

Then Eric had a brainwave. "How about we throw a football match?" he suggested.

"And how are you going to do that, you're rubbish at football" replied Jane

"I've got a betting account" said Eric. Jane raised an eyebrow. "It's only ever got a few quid in it. I bet on football scores, accumulators, that kind of thing. I'm not very good at it but it makes some of the more boring matches a bit more interesting" he confessed. Eric continued: "If we can stick some bets on a penalty being missed at a football match, and somehow I can engineer that to happen then we'd be quids in. Obviously we can't use my online account, but we can visit bookmakers. There's loads around here".

Jane didn't look convinced. Not convinced at all. "So all you have to do is get undetected into a football ground filled with people, sneak onto the pitch, trip up a fast, fit and muscular professional athlete while making it look like someone else had done it and then somehow put off a £50m striker who was paid the equivalent of our mortgage every week to score goals for a living from twelve yards? And this will be achieved by the great Berkshire bucket collector? Yeah, that sounds an absolute piece of piss". Eric conceded that Jane made an excellent point, but it was, by far, the most workable plan they had come up with.

Eric tried to find a match that wasn't being shown on live TV. Liverpool v Brighton was the following weekend and seemed perfect. The odds for a penalty being missed in the game seemed great. 12/1. So, for a grand's investment, Eric calculated they would make twelve thousand pounds profit.

"Put a single bet on the match saying a penalty will be missed. It's really simple"

"How do I put a bet on?" asked Jane. "Shall I use your phone?". Eric was often surprised at his wife's naivety.

"No Jane, this needs to be totally untraceable" Eric explained. They sat in the kitchen and Eric showed Jane how to put on a bet, what to write on the slip and then used Jane's phone to search for the addresses of bookmakers she should visit, with a promise to delete her history once she had visited each one.

Jane agreed to put ten bets of £100 each at ten different bookmakers on the morning of the match.

On the Saturday morning Eric left home at 4am and headed out on the M4 which was beautifully and surprisingly empty. Still miles of roadworks with no sign of any road being worked on, still with a 50mph average speed zone but he was able to cruise serenely all the way to Euston station where he parked in a nearby car park. Eric paid for twenty-four hours of parking, and prayed this would work given how much he was being charged for the privilege of storing his car in an empty basement. Wearing a baseball cap, hoodie and glasses you wouldn't have guessed an invisible man was driving the bland silver Ford Focus and no-one gave him a second glance. However, Eric knew this disguise wouldn't work on a train so reluctantly undressed before he slid out of the car, locking it and leaving the key on top of one of the wheels before carefully walking in the chilly morning air to the platform, vaulting the ticket barrier and sneaking undetected into the last carriage of the 7am express to Liverpool.

Eric found an empty seat in the freshly cleaned carriage in first class and settled in. Eric didn't often use the trains and was soon bored. He didn't want to risk finding a discarded newspaper to read to pass the time even though no-one was around. Eric noticed the omni-present security cameras and although he was convinced no-one would be watching he just didn't want to take the risk. Normally he'd have spent the three hour journey scrolling mindlessly through his phone but instead had to look out of the window and watch England's identikit towns whizz by. They all looked the same. A supermarket, a petrol station, a pub, thousands of houses with thousands of satellite dishes bolted onto the side. Parks with early joggers and dog walkers. It was hypnotically boring and Eric soon found himself drifting off.

He woke with a start at Runcorn. The beeping sound of the train doors being closed snapped him awake. Eric opened his eyes to be greeted by a large, well-dressed woman sitting opposite him, looking him dead in the eye and angrily barking in his direction "hello…can you hear me?".

The fuzzy head one gets from waking up from a power nap disappeared in an instant. Shit. Eric started to flap. He looked down and still couldn't see his legs or body. His mind was racing. Had he left his glasses or cap on? Had he been snoring? She spoke again "hello…?"

Eric was just about to offer a panicked answer when she flicked her hair from her ear and he spotted the Bluetooth headset and the phone in her hand. She hung up and redialled. This time, the person she was calling could hear her and - unfortunately for both Eric and the caller – they were regaled with a long but extraordinarily detailed description of the menstrual cramps she was suffering from that morning and how it was all the fault of the rice cakes she had been eating for breakfast. Eric sat in frozen silence, barely daring to breathe. The conversation lasted all the way until the train pulled into Liverpool's Lime Street station just before 9am. Eric sat and waited until he was sure he was the last passenger left on the train before slowly getting up and slipping through the doors and onto the empty platform.

He calculated that he had five hours to walk the two miles to the ground. There were signposts everywhere so it was easy enough to find the stadium. It was nestled in-between rows and rows of terraced houses, almost appearing out of nowhere as he turned a corner. It was bigger than he'd imagined and he was grateful he'd got there nice and early and there weren't tens of thousands of fans streaming to get in or it would have been impossible to navigate his way into the ground without bumping into people, so narrow were the streets.

Eric found it easy enough to sneak past the handful of stewards and police as he walked round to the player's entrance where the gates were helpfully wide open and 'guarded' by a steward who was barely awake and whose job appeared to be glancing at the ID badges of the TV crews who were bustling about and setting up to cover the match which would be on telly later that night. He wandered down the tunnel past the dressing rooms and through the labyrinth of passages inside the bowels of the stadium and eventually spilled out onto the pitch. Eric walked around on the empty grass a few times to get his bearings and was glad to be moving as he was still a little stiff from the long train ride. He decided to have a look around the stadium, dropping into the changing rooms and then into the director's box where he devoured a couple of the prawn sandwiches that had been left out for the great and the good. Time passed quickly enough and eventually, at 2:30pm, Eric sat himself on the grass right behind a goal while the teams warmed up.

At 3pm the referee's whistle blew and the match began. Eric watched from his prime position and found the game to be amazing. It was fast and furious and the players ran at a pace far faster than he'd imagined. He was worried he'd get trampled on if he wasn't careful, so he decided to wait until the end of the first half when the pace was likely to drop so he could jump out of the way if required. The plan seemed much easier last night when they were discussing it at the dinner table.

Contriving the penalty was surprisingly easy. Eric figured that Liverpool often got penalties at home, and as a player darted through towards the goal he decided to take his chance. Eric waited until the last defender was about to make a tackle when he stuck a leg out as the attacker raced past him and ankle tapped the winger. Down he went like an Olympic diver. Penalty. Nailed on. The crowd went mad, the ref looked nervous but pointed to the spot. He obviously had doubts, but figured getting it wrong in favour of the home team would probably save him from going home in an ambulance. Suddenly, a voice boomed over the stadium PA system. "Video Assistant Referee check complete". No penalty. The crowd groaned and the referee brandished a yellow card to the striker for the blatant dive.

The plan was unravelling fast. Eric gulped hard. He had totally forgotten than all penalties were now reviewed by a video referee. He stood behind the goal and his shoulder slumped. This had been a total waste of time, and now they were £1,000 down. As he cursed his stupidity, he debated just heading home but figured he'd stay and pray for a miracle.

The miracle came midway through the second half. Eric had used half time to walk to the other end of the pitch and again waited for his chance.

The same striker who Eric had tripped earlier hit a fizzing shot and it seemed to strike a defender on the hand while he was protecting his face. Eric thought nothing of it until he heard a shrill blast on a whistle and the saw the referee pointing to the spot. The crowd held it's collective breath while the video referee did his thing, before the announcement came over the loudspeakers. "Video assistant referee check complete. Decision, penalty". The last syllable was drowned out by a deafening roar.

The striker picked up the ball and put it confidently on the penalty spot. Eric made his way back onto the pitch and stood halfway between the player and the ball. He waited until he was running past on his way to take it and said in a strong, clear voice "miss it, you cheating twat". Astonishingly, Eric judged it perfectly. He spoke the words just as the striker had gone past where Eric was standing and the player half-turned to look for who'd spoken to him. This change in momentum happened just as he reached the ball, and at that point it was simply too great to stop and as he connected his body angle was all wrong. The ball went high. Over the bar. Over the stand. It could still be going now, for all Eric knew.

Eric legged it. He was at the tunnel as the chorus of groans cascaded down from the terraces. He was past the dressing rooms and out into the players' car park, running past security and police who had no idea he was even there. No dogs this time, thankfully. Eric nervously jogged the two miles easily enough, glancing back over his shoulder as he went but no-one followed him. He was back at the station and on a train home before the game had ended. Of course, Liverpool won 4-0, but he knew there was no chance their star striker would be talking about "floating voices" when explaining why he'd missed the penalty. As it turned out, he said he thought he'd heard a referee's whistle. Yeah, good one. 'And you're still a cheating twat', thought Eric.

Eric was home by 10pm. Jane was sitting on the couch with three piles of money on the coffee table in front of her. Well over £12,000 worth too, he noticed. Match of the day was on the TV in the lounge and they were showing the handball decision in super slow-motion. Eric could see where he had been standing as the penalty was taken and saw the player turn to look right where he was standing. It was very unnerving.

"Good day at work darling? Asked Jane mischievously

"Oh you know, the usual, traffic was rubbish, Sue from accounts is pregnant again, I made a footballer miss a penalty in front of sixty thousand people and the photocopier got jammed" replied Eric with a grin.

"Sue from accounts is pregnant? We should get her a card" laughed Jane.

"That looks like more than twelve grand Jane" said Eric, fingering the notes.

"Ah, well" said Jane. "I managed to get the first few bets on nice and early, and it was so simple I figured I could do a few more than the ones we agreed so I kind of kept going. I counted them this evening and think I visited about thirty, all in neighbouring towns. And yes, I wore a disguise, and no, I didn't take the car, I took buses, and I've already collected almost all the winnings. I figured I should do this before anyone had noticed".

Eric was speechless. This was beyond his wildest dreams but he knew there could be questions asked if the bookmakers got together. He hugged Jane tightly and whispered "well done my angel" in her ear. But he made a mental note to remind her to stick to the plan next time.

Twelve

Eric and Jane were no experts in money laundering, but they were surprised to find that £36,000 in cash is actually quite a small bundle of bank notes.

They decided to keep it hidden in the vegetable rack. There would be no chance the kids would ever look in there, and use some of the cash rather than spend what they had in the bank. The first priority was to make a secret donation to the crisis centre Jane worked in. The next night, they drove to the centre, stuffed half the money into a carrier bag and Eric scribbled a note using his left hand which read *"thanks for everything you do, you have saved my life"*. He carefully tiptoed out of the car and dropped the bag through the letterbox. The feeling of elation at this good deed spread through his body and Eric felt truly happy. He promised himself he would do more altruistic acts whenever he could, but he still was grateful for the money they hadn't given away. It meant stuff like shopping, petrol, Christmas presents, the day to day stuff that and ordinary life costs were sorted. They had a little bit of cash saved but if they could do this every couple of months they could both quit our jobs and live meaningful lives.

Eric emailed his boss and told him he wasn't coming back. He advised that he simply couldn't work his notice due to stress and anxiety and Eric hoped the company would respect his privacy. The world of call centres would somehow have to cope without him. A reply landed in minutes, thanking Eric for his service and advising that they were about to relocate the call centre to India anyway, so it was all probably for the best.

Jane called her boss and told him she had to stay home and nurse her poor husband back to health and she could perhaps work part time for a month and leave. Her boss was terribly upset, but she did excitedly mention a substantial anonymous donation which they could use to recruit another staff member, and hopefully more donations would follow. Jane said that she hoped that they would, and Eric knew she meant it.

Eric was sitting at the dinner table scouring the Sunday sports section of the newspapers for more ideas on which events he could influence when Oscar and Kate burst through the door. Jane's sister had clearly had enough of looking after two teenagers and had dropped them off and made a run for the hills.

Jane hugged them tightly. It had only been a week since they had left but Eric felt a pang of regret that he couldn't even acknowledge their presence, let alone show any affection.

"Mum, where's Dad?" asked Oscar.

"Oh you know Dad" replied Jane, "off on one of his bloody conferences with the company.

"When's he back?" asked Kate. Eric's heart swelled with pride. They did love their dad and they missed him. He hadn't heard either child say this in some time, and was utterly thrilled that they were asking after him.

"Ummm, a week on Friday" replied Jane, panicking and throwing an arbitrary date into the conversation. She threw Eric a conspiratorial look.

"Excellent" said Kate, "I wanted to have some friends over this weekend and I don't want HIM acting all weird around them like he normally does"

Oscar looked a little more upset and then picked up the newspaper from the dining room table. Eric was sitting less than a yard away as he did so. "Mum, what are you doing reading this?" he asked. "You hate sport. This is Dad's paper".

Jane flushed. "He wanted me to record the football later and I was just checking what time it started". The lie came far too easily. "Anyway, it's supper time soon, so go and wash your hands and lay the table".

Placated, Oscar replied "Great, what are we having?"

"Roast beef sandwiches" replied Jane. The kids exchanged a nervous glance. "we're not hungry" they replied in unison, and scuttled off to bed.

Eric leaned back in his chair. "It is odd to hear your kids talk about you when they don't know you can see and hear them. I assumed they had enough going on in their lives to worry about me, but it was a little disappointing that Oscar didn't even question it when he heard I'd gone without saying goodbye. And what the hell does Kate mean by 'acting weird?' I don't act weird, do I?".

"Keep your voice down, they'll hear you" whispered Jane. "You don't act weird but you tell a lot of very bad dad jokes. I'm sure that's what she meant".

Eric wasn't convinced, but decided to let it pass. They figured they would need to tell their children eventually, but not yet. They were decidedly ambivalent about their Dad's unexpected departure, much to Eric's disappointment.

The next few weeks were tremendously exciting for them both. Jane used a variety of disguises and they visited lots of different towns, putting on bets which Eric's invisibility could influence. It was enlightening the myriad ways someone invisible could manipulate a sporting result.

What Eric really wanted to do was not necessarily change the outcome per se, but make a few quid from predicting something that happened within the event. In-play betting, he now knows it to be called.

Being unseen was about to finally prove advantageous.

Thirteen

The plan started in earnest at the Reading Masters snooker tournament, which was being held only about eight miles from the Eric's home town so they were relieved to discover there was no need to spend hours bored senseless on a train in the fear of being sat on. The top seed and current World Champion had cruised to the semi-final and was a clear favourite to beat his unseeded opponent. Eric decided to bet on him only making one century break in the match. Although the odds weren't brilliant, they were still generous enough and it felt an easy one to pull off. Eric had repeated his Anfield trick of getting to the town nice and early and parking in an underground car park before the walk to the venue, breezing undetected through open doors and hiding himself under the table while waiting for the fun to begin. There were far less security guards and police officers surrounding the conference hall where the tournament was being played than there had been in Liverpool but he was still careful to keep close to the walls of the corridors and avoid any areas where people were starting to assemble.

What seemed like many hours later lights started flickering into life and the audience began filing in. Another hour or so later the referee appeared and Eric could hear him putting the balls on their spots before a very enthusiastic Master of Ceremonies breathlessly introduced the gladiatorial protagonists in bow ties and three-piece suits. The crowd whooped with joy, and Eric couldn't help thinking they needed to get out more.

Eric found snooker a boring enough game while watching it on TV, and lying on a thin and itchy carpet, while the 'action' went on above him hadn't made him change his mind. The match began and soon enough he could hear the referee calling out the scores of each break as balls clacked together and dropped into pockets. Eric was just able to see the electronic scoreboard too, so it was easy enough to judge when he'd need to make his move.

The matched plodded along and it was clear the champion was in imperious form, rattling in a century in the second frame, just needing three more frames to win.

At four-nil and with the champion only needing one more frame for an easy win Eric began to relax. Groans from the crowd told him that he was in an impossible position, but then after a crash of balls from above his head the spectators went apoplectic. It turns out he'd smashed into the pack of balls on the table, one had fortuitously spilled into a pocket and the rest had fallen perfectly for him and, naturally, left him firmly on course for his second century break of the match. Eric had to act. He considered tying the player's shoelaces together, stealing his chalk or putting his hand over a pocket to prevent a ball from dropping but these didn't seem practical when the time came. So, on the ninth black Eric silently climbed out from under the table, crept up next to him and blew gently in his ear, causing him to miss the shot by some distance. He spun round, startled and swatted away an imaginary fly. By this point, he was so far ahead anyway his opponent immediately conceded the frame, and the match. No harm done, and another ten thousand pounds in the kitty.

Eric drove home and parked the car as usual a few streets away, sneaking into his own house was a hassle but having the kids ask questions about why the car was on the drive when Dad wasn't home would have been awkward to say the least. Eric could only enter through the back door and would wait until he was sure the children were asleep before coming inside. He made sure he only left once they'd gone to school. He was, for the first time, really starting to miss them.

Eric waited for Jane's text to confirm the kids were asleep when he snuck inside. The match had finished quite late and all the bookmakers were closed, so Jane would need to go and collect the winnings in the morning. Eric spoke first:

"Ten thousand? That about right?"

"Yep" said Jane. "I'll grab it in the morning and we can drop half at the shelter tomorrow night"

Eric paused. This had been on his mind for a few days. "Look Jane, the stuff we're doing for your centre is great, and it makes me happy that we're helping, but.."

Jane cut him off. "No Eric. Fifty – fifty. We keep half to help with the mortgage, and they get half to make sure they can stay afloat"

"Yeah but how much more do we need to do?" Eric knew he was treading a fine line here but could already smell the leather of the Porsche he'd be buying once the mortgage was paid off. Eric had worked the numbers while sitting under the snooker table. And he could see lots of zeros. "Charity begins at home Jane. We've already given them so much, probably more than they can spend. Think of the good we could do for the kids with the extra money"

Jane fixed her husband with a steely stare. "Don't turn into an arsehole Eric. We're not petty thieves. We do this and help people and keep some for ourselves, or we don't do it at all".

Eric knew when to shut the fuck up. This was one of those times.

Fourteen

The next opportunity came at the British Grand Prix. The public's favourite racer, a true British superstar, was on pole, leading the championship standings and looking uncatchable. Jane drove Eric up to Silverstone early on the Sunday of the race, dropping him off at a pub in Towcester which was a mile or so from the circuit, before heading away to place bets on him simply not winning which on current form was unthinkable. She then agreed that she would return to the pub and sit to wait for her brave returning all-conquering husband. Well, those were Eric's words, not hers.

Even though they arrived shortly after dawn, the paths leading to the track were very busy with eager spectators who were being herded by stewards into long snaking queues for ticket and bag checks. Many of the fans were carrying cooler boxes and camping chairs and slipping past them without bumping into a few would be impossible. The track was surrounded by a twelve foot fence, so it took some time to work out how to get inside unnoticed. Eric circumnavigated the venue until he stumbled across the Corporate Hospitality entrance. There was no need for the great and the good to arrive so early and queue with the common people, so that was his opportunity. He slipped under the boom gate and walked through the tunnel that heads under the track and into the central paddock.

Eric recognised the multitude of gleaming trucks and Winnebagos, all lined up neatly together and decked out in the colours of the various teams and plastered in advertising logos of oil companies and IT conglomerates. Some of the team crews were already scuttling around, all with headphones on and clutching various pieces of expensive carbon fibre with lanyards and security passes flapping around their necks. The paddock itself was much bigger than he had imagined, although it was easy enough to navigate through and drop down an unguarded staircase which led him away from the trucks and into the garages where the cars were sitting silently, belying the excitement and energy that would propel them around the track in just a few hours' time.

Eric crept through what he calculated to be the middle garage and positioned himself by a gap on the pit wall between two teams and opposite our superstar's car which was located right on the other side of the pit lane and waited.

He was in his position at 9am, and the race started at 2pm. Eric steeled himself for five hours of boredom. He watched the day slowly build around him and by 12pm the garages and paddock were a hive of activity. The noise of cars being fired up and revved was deafening and Eric noted enviously how everyone was wearing headphones to dampen the sound. He sat with his hands over his ears but the angry screaming of engines was giving him a thumping headache. 'I'm not doing this next year', he promised himself.

As the start of the race approached the pit lane was mobbed with people. There were camera crews, celebrities and mechanics, all jostling for position around the drivers and their cars. Eric eased himself up and stood against the fence on top of the pit wall, being careful not to either lose his balance and fall head first into a TV crew or slip backwards and land on the actual track, almost certainly breaking an ankle in the fall. He watched as famous actors aggressively pushed past mechanics just to be seen on television and realised the slick production you saw when the race was televised masked the chaos of real life.

Eventually, the track cleared and the race got underway. The noise reduced as the cars sped away and became more tolerable as they started to spread out. From his position on the pit wall, Eric turned and watched the cars scream past, while also keeping an eye on the garages to make sure he could calculate the path he'd need to take to get in and out to complete his task. Watching a car go past at 200mph was initially thrilling, but by the fourth time they'd been round the track and past the start line he was thoroughly bored with the race and turned his attention to the tyres and tools that were so neatly stacked in the garages.

With the race approaching halfway, Eric scooted across to the pit garage and found a small, but very pointy screwdriver from a tool box and jammed it into the two sets of spare front left tyres that were waiting to be selected, covered in little heating mats like the world's most expensive pigs in blankets. The unmistakable hissing noise wasn't heard by anyone but Eric over the sounds of the engines, and Eric quickly placed the screwdriver back in the tool box and darted back to the pit wall narrowly avoiding being run over by the guy coming dead last which Eric mused would have been very humiliating indeed, and he sat to watch the fun unfold.

Several minutes later, the helmeted pit crew leapt into life, each grabbing a tyre with a man at the front with a jack assuming the now familiar position to hoist the car up and change the wheels in milliseconds. But as the car skidded to a stop, the mechanic with the front left tyre ran back into the garage, hurling his wheel into the tool box with such force it flew everywhere, spilling its contents all over the floor. He picked up the second tyre and could immediately feel it was flat too. Panic broke out throughout the crew, with the team boss remonstrating with everyone else and clearly asking what the hell was going on.

The driver sat, engine revving, gesticulating wildly at his crew and banging the cockpit in frustration. By now the crew were pushing and shoving each other in total disarray and Eric could see the giant leaderboard on the main straight with the British number one falling further and further down the standings as everyone else whizzed by.

Eric knew that by the time they'd managed to pinch the teams' other driver's tyres the local hero would be too far down the field to get back into contention, and so it proved. He speed-walked up the track to the end of the pit lane and skirted the paddock building until Eric found a small wall to jump over away from the marshals and speeding cars. By now, everyone was clamouring to see what had caused the delay and were focused on the angry exchanges inside the garage. Eric figured he could have walked away unnoticed if he were wearing a bright yellow hazmat suit and a luminous balaclava, such was the attention on the mechanics' volcanic argument. The last image he saw as he turned to leave the pit lane was a series of punches being thrown and the team's second driver almost rear-ending the stationary car as he skidded to a stop. When he discovered his tyres were being fitted to his championship rival's car Eric assumed it would lead to a meltdown of biblical proportions.

Eric retraced his steps back to the Corporate Hospitality exit and calmly walked through the car park, past all the road legal Aston Martins, McLarens and Ferraris towards the main gate. As agreed, he headed back to the pub car park where he'd been dropped earlier that morning and let himself into Jane's car before the race was over. Eric grabbed his phone from the glove box and pinged her a text to let her know he was there. Eric could see Jane sitting at a table in the beer garden, and watched as she finished her lime and soda in one long gulp and soon enough they were on the M40 heading home with about thirty five thousand pounds of winnings to be collected the following week.

Eric had the numbers in his head. "Seventeen grand, that's a lot of money we're giving away" he said.

Jane gripped the wheel tightly. "I know Eric. I know".

Eric smiled to himself. He knew the nut was beginning to crack.

Fifteen

Next, cricket. Eric quite liked cricket but Jane never understood the game. 'Far too long, far too boring and how can modern professional sportsmen still get excited about tea?' she would moan whenever it was on TV. Eric played it a bit in his youth and knew this should be an easy-ish one to accomplish. He made his way to the Rose Bowl in Southampton for a four-day county match, but this time getting in was even more of a doddle than before. There were more players on the pitch than fans in the stands, and he ambled past a semi-conscious steward who was more interested in the contents of his nose than a pitch invasion from the empty seats behind him. England's top test bowler was playing, and making his first appearance after a long injury. Knowing he'd be as rusty as hell, Jane had, as instructed, backed him bowling his first bowl as a no-ball which would be highly unusual for him, but explainable given the circumstances. Eric had given up trying to explain to Jane what a no-ball was and why they sometimes just happened.

It was an overcast, chilly day. More clouds than blue sky. The umpire seemed to have three jerseys and two coats on and looked about as excited to be there as the security guard.

As England's finest steamed in to deliver his first ball, Eric positioned himself right behind the umpire and as he hit his delivery stride he gave the bowler the gentlest of nudges in his back. This projected him forward just enough to cause him to lose his balance and he hurled the ball, head-high with equal measures of alarm on both his, and the batsman's faces who deftly rocked back and let the ball steam violently into the wicketkeeper's gloves with a reassuring "thwack".

"No-ball" shouted the umpire. "No-shit" replied the batsman. The bowler looked around for someone to blame, and figuring the umpire was unlikely to have been the one to administer a gentle shove, shook his head and kicked at an imaginary divot.

By now, Eric and Jane had expanded their footprint and were putting bets on across three counties. It took three days to visit all the towns and cities to lay the bets, and another three to collect the winnings. Long odds and small stakes were still the order of the day to avoid arousing suspicion. The cricket episode returned sixty thousand pounds. Eric decided to just let the money sit on the table in a big pile and say nothing. Jane's eyes were wide enough, and he knew she was starting to think about whether the charity really needed even more cash than they'd already donated. Still, and reluctantly, half was put in a bag and dropped through the letterbox.

Next up was the Welsh Open golf tournament. Eric found a green where a hole-in-one was most likely, and positioned himself three yards from the flag. Altogether Eric and Jane stuck fifty grand on there being at least one hole-in-one at the tournament and nudging the first ball into the hole that was tracking the cup was a doddle. And the golfer won a car for his troubles too, which was nice for him. Fifty grand at four to one. That returned two hundred thousand pounds.

At home, with Jane counting the pile of money, Eric spoke. "we're going to get caught soon enough if we keep dropping piles of banknotes through that letterbox. They're going to be setting up cameras to find out who's being so generous. And that will lead to questions about where the money is coming from".

Jane started to protest but she knew he was right.

In all, and after just four weeks of effort, Eric and Jane had cleared over £390,000. They'd dropped £70,000 into Jane's shelter and had to move the bulging carrier bag of cash from the vegetable rack and into a disused watering can in the shed. Even Oscar and Kate would eventually notice a bag starting to spill its contents of used twenties amongst the parsnips and carrots.

Eric and Jane finally decided that was enough money for now, and they had taken the requisite number risks without being caught. They scoured the papers and internet, but couldn't find any news of a betting scam. They had been careful. Jane always wore a different disguise including wigs, glasses, clothes and put the bets on at different times to ensure there were no patterns. There were no stakes of more than £100, and just enough losing bets to create confusion. Now £300,000 in banknotes is quite a large amount of money, so it got bundled up and hidden in the shed in the aforementioned cobweb covered watering can. Long since cleared of chemicals, the kids had refused to go in there so they guessed it would be safe enough. A new padlock was bought for the shed door however.

Sixteen

On the Monday following the golf tournament Jane sat the kids down at the breakfast table. They still hadn't figured out how to explain Eric's invisibility, but knew they had to eventually. Just not yet. Eric stood by the back door. He wanted to hear their reactions for himself.

Jane cleared her throat. "Dad's been asked to go to India to help set up the new call centre. We think he'll be there for a month or so. He is at the airport now waiting for a flight. He did say he was sorry and would call you when he's landed".

Eric was secretly thrilled when Oscar started crying at this news, and even Kate looked upset, whining "But we miss him, please tell him to hurry home. It's not fair. He hates that stupid job".

Eric started to feel real regret. He had begun to really pay attention to the kids, watching them sleep and even sitting near the dinner table while they chatted to Jane about their days. They loved their new phones they'd been given and had sent Eric a load of texts to say thank you. Eric had made sure his phone was always on silent and stashed in his bedside drawer when he wasn't out manipulating sporting events.

Kate suddenly looked up and announced "Hey, our new phones can track Dad's. Let's see where he is!" As she reached for her phone to open the tracking app, Eric sprinted through the kitchen, up the stairs and managed to flick his phone to airplane mode before it started pinging and giving the game away.

Panting on the bed, Eric could hear the puzzled chatter from Kate below.

"It says his last location is here Mum, how can that be?"

Jane was never a confident or comfortable liar, but the last few weeks of subterfuge and deception had begun to change her moral compass and she didn't pause for breath, replying "he left so early this morning that he forgot to charge it, I am sure he'll charge it when he's on the plane. I'll get him to call you both as soon as he can to let you know he's safe". This seemed to pacify the kids for the moment.

Eric listened from the bedroom. He had already resolved to be a better dad once this was all over. He'd really neglected the kids over the past few years and promised to use the money they'd made to give them a better life, but more importantly to spend time with them. He was starting to see the irony of believing himself invisible for the past twenty years, yet he had the power all along to do something about it. Now, and for the first time since he'd become invisible, he started to feel real regret at what he'd been missing.

That week Oscar was picked for the school football team, and Eric knew he had to go and watch. He had missed so many matches because of work and now finally had the chance to go and support his son, albeit from a distance and without Oscar knowing. But Eric would know and that felt like a start. On the day of the game he disrobed and started walking towards the school. When he was a hundred yards away he suddenly realised he would be standing amongst a group of children completely undressed. Despite his need to support his lad, he knew this wasn't right and felt deeply uncomfortable. He cursed, turned on his heels and headed home.

Eric still had no thought as to how this would end but figured he'd need to either find a cure, or tell them. He couldn't be traveling for work for ever. How many call centre conventions and new office openings could there be? And having attended many over the years, he could happily attest to the fact that one was one too many.

Seventeen

Eric decided to channel his frustration and used this time to settle some scores. They were sure they now had enough money and he was becoming bored of sneaking round the house and calling the kids from the garage while pretending to be in some exotic conference hall, so Eric started lying awake at night, thinking of who'd wronged him in the past and how he could seek a modicum of revenge. He knew this was childish and petty but he also knew that he might never get another chance to get some closure on events of the past.

Ben Jones had beaten Eric up at school thirty-five years ago because he'd "looked at him funny". He was a proper old-school bully. A crew-cutted, knuckle-dragging thug from the dodgy side of town who had smacked pretty much every kid in their year during a very undistinguished educational career. Knowing he'd risen to the dizzying heights of local bus driver, he was easy enough to find. He drove the number eleven which went from the centre of town to the council estate and back again, a dozen times a day. The route passed about a mile from the Curtis house, and Eric had seen him drive past many times, deliberately hitting puddles to soak pedestrians or simply ignoring bus stops with schoolkids desperate to get home. 'Once a prick, always a prick', Eric thought to himself.

He walked down to the bus stop and waited. His was the third bus to come past but by now Eric had got used to hanging around and the hour or so it took for him to appear was nothing compared to sitting on a pit wall at Silverstone for five hours. He stopped to let a middle aged lady off the bus and Eric slipped in before the doors closed, making sure it was just the two of them left aboard. As Jones eased into the traffic he grabbed his mobile phone and began tapping away at the keys, half an eye on the road but paying more attention to the message he was sending. Eric gripped the handrail next to the driver's cab as tightly as he could, and yanked the steering wheel to the left, sending his bus crashing into a line of parked cars. Naturally, Eric punched him hard in the face as the bus came to a stop for good measure. Eric hit the door release button and tiptoed through the broken glass, onto the pavement and home, giggling to himself every step of the way.

A few days later, Eric went to his first place of work to see Mr Stark, who was the manager of the local department store where he'd been a young trainee. His first proper job. Eric really liked working there and was earning reasonable money for an eighteen year old. It allowed him to start living independently, and it made his parents proud of him too. Eric had begun saving to move into a flat and was ready to take on the world. But as his manager, Stark had fired Eric for threatening to expose him for stealing from the Christmas party fund. He'd said Eric would never get a reference if he told anyone, and, being eighteen, Eric had had believed him. It was devastating. Eric had to abandon his plans to move out and ended up, covered in shame and embarrassment, working in a bloody call centre, which set him on a career path that would result in him, thirty two years later, eating boring sandwiches under fluorescent lights in Chiswick.

It was the first time Eric had been back there since that day, but he knew he was still the manager there. They'd probably bury the creepy old bastard in the lingerie department. Eric walked into the store and it didn't take long to find him, stalking the shop floor and peering at everyone suspiciously over his glasses. Dressed in his usual three-piece suit Eric started to follow him trying to pick his moment. He waited for Stark to walk past a large porcelain figurine display when he shoved him, hard. He fell, arms and legs flailing, into the glass shelves, destroying thousands of pounds worth of stock. He went down in super-slow motion, the look of bewilderment, embarrassment and surprise on his face was an utter joy to behold. As he struggled to his feet with the help of customers and subservient staff Eric noticed a large gash on his head. He whispered "Merry Christmas you old fucker" into his ear as he crept away.

Eric was on a roll. This felt good. A hard knock life of perceived injustices was being corrected, and he was unleashing many years of frustration and resentment.

Next, it was the turn of the Finance Director of the call centre company Eric had just worked for. The job had been ok, most of the people had been ok, but Kenny Sinclair had been an almighty bastard. Hateful, horrible, spiteful and penny-pinching. Eric's boss was the Operations Director, and he was a just about bearable. An old man in a hurry to retire, so largely left him alone - but Eric had been on weekly Zoom calls for a year with the Finance Director, and he was one of those people who was never satisfied. His negotiations with Eric on staff pay was the tip of an unpleasant iceberg, with Stark openly admitting he'd make everyone redundant in heartbeat if he could automate the answering of the phones. Relocating the call centre to India was a dream come true, but naturally Stark's was the one job that would be safe.

He had a Scrooge McDuck poster on his wall, with the mean old trouserless bastard glaring out over a pile of money with the caption "bigger, better, faster, cheaper" emblazoned underneath like his own personal mantra. Every call would be a shouting match with Sinclair berating everyone at a slightly lower level than him. Even if all targets were met, and all profit forecasts exceeded he'd complain that the team had fucked something up because "you hairy-arsed call handlers can't get anything right". So sneaking into his office at 2am one morning and dropping a bag of Toto's 'garden delights' on his desk was a lovely moment. Eric had been collecting them for a month or so, and the smell was making him retch and giggle in equal measure. Toto didn't deliver much, but a dog-egg twice a day in the garden was about the only thing you could rely on him for. His one redeeming feature. It could have been quite the party trick, if they ever had friends round.

Eric drove to the office, his heart singing at the realisation of the journey that he now didn't have to make through necessity of paying the mortgage. He parked a few roads away from the office, opening the boot and picking up the carrier bag which seemed to omit a gentle hum from the three kilos of dog shit inside and walked through the familiar car park which no longer had his name and job title stencilled on the wall. Eric skirted round the building to the warehouse at the back, hoping they still hadn't fixed the lock and knowing the alarm wouldn't be activated because no-one could remember the code. The door opened and no siren sounded. He was in.

Eric walked up the three flights of stairs, relieved that no nostalgia for the old days came flooding through his veins. Just a sense of bitter regret he'd wasted so long doing this for a living. The smell of despair and acceptance of a life poorly lived almost overpowered the smell of his carrier bag. Almost, but not quite. The building was being shut down ahead of the impending move to India. Staff desks had been dismantled and were stacked against the wall, the computers servers were all unplugged and the coffee machine had been removed. But the executive offices were still there.

Eric found Sinclair's office, pushed the door open with his elbow and wandered over to his desk. He unloaded Toto's leaving gift all over the keyboard, chair and desk, and used Sinclair's monogrammed Mont-Blanc pen to smear a brown comedy moustache on Scrooge's bill on the poster on the wall. The smell made Eric gag and he just wished he could have been there to see his tormentor's face when he next arrived at work. Eric could imagine it though, and knew he'd be beyond incandescent with rage. He momentarily felt sorry for the few operations staff who were still working there as he knew their lives would be hell for a few weeks, but Eric knew it was worth it for the pain and misery he's inflicted on so many people over the years.

Finally, and most satisfyingly, Eric went to Dave Treville's motor dealership one Friday night. An emporium of bollocks, if ever there was one. He'd bought a car along with a "cast-iron, no limit, unconditional warranty" from him many years ago when he couldn't really afford it. Unbelievably, Eric had fallen for the sales patter which included something about how he was reluctant to sell it at all as he wanted to keep the car for his daughter. Unsurprisingly, it turned out to be a giant pile of shit. It had broken down two weeks after Eric had taken delivery while he had been out on a date with Jane. It was winter, in the middle of nowhere and they had ended up walking miles just to get a phone signal to call for help. They had no real idea where they were and how to give directions for the tow truck. The car was hissing and steaming and it was clear the head gasket had blown. Eventually, the recovery truck had arrived at around 6am, and they towed the car and their cold passengers back to Treville's garage. They got there just as he was opening up in the morning. Treville watched as the car was lowered off the back of the pick-up and he loudly announced that because the roadside mechanic had "fucked about with it" no warranty would be valid and Eric should 'piss off before he bounced him down the street'.

Eric duly fucked off, tail between his legs and he became the proud owner of a car that even the local council didn't want as practice for the fire brigade. It cost him about as much to have it scrapped as he'd paid for it, and almost a year to finish clearing the debt at a time they could least afford it. And he was still out there, selling cars and being a colossal prick about it.

So, with one last big score to settle, Eric took a box of matches over to his dealership, and, after breaking a window of a twenty year old Ford Cortina, unlocked the car and opened the fuel cap, and then dropped the lit match into the petrol tank. Eric scarpered to a safe distance across the street. The whole lot went up in seconds. He sat and watched as the fire brigade arrived, far too late to save anything of value, and knowing the tight sod wouldn't have insurance. Treville appeared at the same time as the fire brigade and on seeing his worldly possessions go up in flames, dropped to his knees and sobbed. A more mature, grounded and reasonable man would have felt pity for him. Unfortunately for Dave Treville, Eric was beginning to become none of those things and he danced a little jig all the way home.

Eighteen

Eric had no regrets about being vindictive and settling old scores. Everyone he'd targeted over the past week had absolutely deserved it in his opinion. None of them would really remember Eric when he was in their lives, he'd meant very little to them. He had now understood he'd spent his life being unseen and started to enjoy the fact that even if they didn't know who had caused such mayhem, they wouldn't be able to ignore him now.

There was one more pull Eric couldn't resist, especially for a man of his age, one approaching, or maybe even going through, or maybe even just heading past, a mid-life crisis. Obviously, he didn't tell Jane any of this. It's not that she wouldn't approve—maybe she would, it's that he didn't want her to see this side of him. Eric promised himself he'd have one more adventure before becoming the dutiful husband and father he yearned to be. It was something he wanted to do for himself. It was the only chance he was ever going to get, as he knew she would veto splashing their ill-gotten gains in such a manner.

Back in his old life, Eric would occasionally walk past the biggest Porsche dealership in London at lunchtime and stop, munching on his sandwich, nose pressed to the glass like a schoolboy, trying to figure out what colour to get if his lottery numbers came in. The dark blue Porsche 911 was displayed on a revolving plinth, and he would dream of belting down to the South of France in it, sweeping around corners at breathtaking speeds

So late one afternoon, Eric donned his motorbike gear with helmet and gloves and headed into London, and parked a few roads away from the dealership.

Eric slipped into a small park where some bushes provided plenty of cover from the road and got undressed. He jogged round to the Porsche dealership walked inside, and plonked himself down on one of the uncomfortable yet achingly stylish hard leather chairs that are reserved for people who normally pay the equivalent of Eric's weekly salary for an oil change. At 5pm on the dot, the lights started to flicker off and people started to leave. Mechanics, receptionists, shiny-suited sales reps and service assistants. He sat dead still and waited. At just after 6pm all the lights went out and Eric heard the roller shutters closing at the main entrance. He waited another hour. he wanted the A4 to be clear of traffic, as he assumed that alarms would be going mad as he burst through the plate glass windows in the 911 and Eric absolutely wanted to rip this car a new arsehole if he possibly could.

Just after 7pm Eric got up, stretched and looked out of the window at the road outside. Traffic had thinned and there was plenty of room to manoeuvre. He moved over to the sales manager's desk and found the lock box where he kept the keys to the showroom cars. Predictably, it was locked. Also predictably, the key was in the drawer next to it. Obviously having a proper security system was simply a massive pain in the arse and he was as complacent and lazy as every other office manager Eric had ever met, including Eric himself.

Eric opened the box and grabbed a few keys, pressing the unlock buttons until the lights of *his* 911 flashed. Bingo. Eric dropped the rest back in the box and locked it again, making sure he wiped any fingerprints from everything he'd touched. Eric walked over to the service area and picked up a set of thin rubber gloves that the mechanics used and slipped them on, and went over to the main showroom door, trying to figure out how to get the shutter open. He had envisaged smashing through the glass and sliding into the road like James Bond, but now he was actually faced with it, wasn't sure he'd do anything more than smash the shit out of the front of the car, set off the airbag and find himself locked in a Porsche garage for the night. Then he noticed the big red button that said "emergency door release". Instinctively, he pushed it. The doors silkily slid open and the shutter glided up and out of the way. And to Eric's total surprise a flashing red light went off along with a very angry-sounding klaxon.

Eric sprinted to his dream car, tossed the keys into the armrest console, got in behind the wheel and hit the start button, and revved the engine. He flicked the gearbox into first and left two very long, and very satisfying black rubber skid marks from the plinth all the way to the front door. As he looked in the rear view mirror he could see the flashing red light and just about make out the klaxon over the sound of the engine, so he shoved his foot hard onto the loud pedal and headed west, away from London towards more open, forgiving roads.

For the next thirty minutes or so, Eric metaphorically ripped the throat out of this incredible machine. He turned southwest at Richmond and picked up the A316, knowing this was going to be quieter and have a few more twisty roundabouts to enjoy. The dealership had left around a quarter of a tank of petrol in the car, and he guessed that it would be at least thirty minutes before the cops would be awake and alert and able to find him. He planned on using as much of that quarter tank in those thirty minutes as he could.

The A316 is mainly dual carriageway and was beautifully empty. Eventually it turns into the M3 and Eric wanted to hit the Sunbury turn off just before then, dump the car and catch the train back to West London to pick up his bike and get home. Eric accelerated through red lights and made every speed camera on the road flash like he was at a strobe light convention. Engine roaring and wheels squealing. Eric became the type of driver he normally tutted and shook his head at as he drives past when out walking Toto. 'But', thought Eric, 'hypocrisy is a dish best served at breakneck speed in a stolen hundred thousand pound car'.

Eric hit the turn off at around 140mph and skidded to a halt in an unlit car park about half a mile from Sunbury station. He tried to do a few donuts in the car park, but realised he didn't really know how to do them and was, in effect, just driving round in circles and making himself feel queasy. Checking there were no cameras, he killed the engine and stepped out of the car, leaving the keys in the centre consol. Eric could hear the exhausted plinking of the engine and smelt the burning rubber from the tyres. He was full of adrenaline and smiling like an idiot. He could start to hear the faint sounds of sirens which were definitely starting to get closer, so giving the car a friendly tap on the bonnet like they were old mates, he reluctantly headed for the railway station. He took off the latex gloves he'd been wearing and dropped them in a recycling bin of a house he walked past. And then it started to rain.

Ten minutes later, soaked, Eric stepped onto the train that headed back to Chiswick. Mercifully it was empty. He was leaving wet footprints everywhere and was shivering with the cold. He used the seat as a towel and tried to dry himself as best as he could, promising himself a shower in caustic soda when he got home. Christ knew what was in those seats. Tramp piss and sweat, by the smell of things. Soon enough the train pulled into Chiswick station and he made his way to the exit, vaulting the ticket barrier and dodging the handful of office workers who were wearily heading home. Entering the park and moving the branches of the sodden bush aside, Eric found his pile of soaking wet clothes, helmet and facemask and put them on. It was horrible. He was freezing cold and his fingers were numb. It was hard to see through the heavy rain as he pulled the bike out onto the main road as he navigated the roads at a considerably more sedate pace than he'd done an hour or so earlier. Shivering, wet, dicing with death on a bike that was handling like a slippery eel covered in snot, and the biggest, shit-eating grin imaginable across his face. A truly magnificent evening.

Eric got home, parked the bike in the garage and shivered his way up the stairs into a steaming hot shower.

Bliss.

Little did Eric know that everything was about to change. But then, just how long did Eric honestly think being truly unseen would last?

Nineteen

Eric didn't notice the black van parked outside the house on that Friday morning. He was due 'home' on the Saturday and they had resolved to tell the kids what had happened, with the promise of TVs for their bedrooms if they'd kept their mouths shut. Eric was feeling great. They were beginning to think about taking a holiday (somewhere hot, paying cash, private and secluded so Eric could walk around without raising suspicion). Eric opened his front door. He'd decided to sneak a quick drink at the Red Lion, and he paused to breathe in the fresh air. He turned, closing it softly behind him. He was just thinking about how he could travel overseas without being noticed when, out of nowhere, everything went dark.

A bag was pulled over Eric's head and he was hoisted into the air and carried by what felt like several men away from the house. Eric heard the door of a van opening and he was roughly thrown inside.

No words were spoken. No instructions given, either to each other or to their captive. Eric lay, petrified and confused. The floor of the van was rock hard and he'd landed heavily, crying out in pain and reaching to pull his mask from his face when a rough hand batted Eric's arm away. A single word was uttered which reverberated around the interior of the van. "No".

The van started and took off, wheels spinning and engine revving. Eric was absolutely terrified. He began to beg. "Who are you? What do you want?" He hated how pathetic he sounded, but when no reply came, carried on. "I'm sorry. Whatever I've done to upset you, I'm sorry. I'll give it back. All of it". Again, silence. He then tried making a mental note of the route they were taking to try and calculate the destination. This proved impossible as the van was hurtling around roundabouts and making left and right turns at an alarming rate.

Eric tried to compose himself. His mind was racing. Who could have kidnapped him? Who could have known where, or who he was? Whoever had done this was confident enough to snatch him in broad daylight. How had they even seen him?

Eric pushed these thoughts from his mind and tried to think rationally. He was pretty sure whoever had him were either violent and pissed-off bookmakers (that would be bad), a finance director with dog shit under his fingernails (meh) or some clandestine government department and he was about to be rectally probed (which, he opined, was probably the worst of his options).

Eric had no idea how long he was in the van for. Minutes? Hours? He couldn't tell. During the journey his hands had been bound in front of him and his captors had forced him into a pair of tracksuit pants. He was bouncing around the back of the van so resolved to try and lie in the foetal position and wait it out. Still silence from his captors. Not even a radio playing. Eventually, the van skidded to a stop and the door opened. Eric was grabbed again and carried from the van. The noises made him realise they were in a big city. Traffic, sirens and the general hubbub bounced off the walls around him. A door opened and he was carried inside. Eric realised then that these people didn't care that they were probably being seen carrying a man with a bag on his head through city streets in broad daylight and that really started to make him panic. He crossed finance director from his mental list.

Eric was placed upright, and the bag from his head was removed. It took a while for him to adjust his eyes to the fluorescent light and take in his surroundings. Six large men stood around him, all black army fatigues, muscles and tattoos. Eric asked them to untie to his hands. A shake of the head from meat head number one told him they'd stay bound for now. Eric was frogmarched by his captors down several windowless corridors and dumped into what was obviously someone important's office. His hands were finally freed and suddenly he was alone, the door closing silently behind him. The office had a huge window overlooking the Houses of Parliament and a picture of the King adorned the wall. Right, so it probably wasn't the bookmakers, and he was in London, he guessed almost certainly in a government building. There was a large desk and two chairs, one on either side. A mobile phone and laptop were the only items on the desk, so Eric instinctively reached for the phone but it was locked. He was about to slip his tracksuit pants off and see if he could make his escape when he noticed the skin on his stomach had a very fluorescent glow about it.

Eric was starting to flap now. He was clearly in some very deep shit , and the bright yellow paint on his stomach and the clothing they'd forced him into showed him they knew what they were dealing with.

As scenarios ricocheted through Eric's mind, the door opened and being unseen took on a whole new meaning.

Twenty

Andy Barnes was head of MI6. Eric knew his name immediately, because his ID badge said so and it was the first words he'd heard since leaving the house as he introduced himself. He was the definition of Mr Average. 5' 11", medium build, greying hair, no distinguishing features, grey suit. A man you would walk past a hundred times without giving him a second glance. But when he spoke, you knew absolutely that he was the man in charge. He met Eric with an outstretched hand and a confident smile.

"Mr Curtis, lovely to meet you, I've been looking forward to this for some weeks now" he said. "Now, have you been offered a tea or coffee, water, a pint of beer from the Red Lion?"

If this revelation was supposed to strike like a dagger to Eric's heart it worked. However Eric manfully brushed the barb away.

"Coffee, milk and two, strong as you like, please" Eric replied. While he was still in a state of shock, confidently ordering coffee for thirty years was clearly a skill that remained embedded even under extreme pressure. Eric had hoped this would make Barnes realise he was not a man to be fucked with, but in reality his voice sounded weak and shrill as he ordered his drink.

"Of course, on its way" said Andy kindly. Eric looked around. It was just the two of them in the room, so Eric guessed others were listening in to the conversation. This was confirmed when one of the meat heads came in with the coffee less than thirty seconds later. Eric immediately recognised one of the mugs from his own kitchen, as he was sure he was expected to do.

"Paris, France", said Andy, nodding towards Eric's mug. "Lovely in the springtime. I think that's how the song goes. Music was never my forte"

Eric gripped the mug tightly. Kate had bought it for him on a school trip last year and he had drunk his morning coffee from it every day. He loved the kitschness of it and although the Eiffel Tower was starting to fade, it was one of his most treasured possessions.

Andy noticed the alarm in Eric's eyes. "Don't worry, they're fine" he said. "Even the dog - he's a lively one, isn't he. Toto, isn't it?". This felt to Eric like being on an episode of Derren Brown. If his ability to anticipate his questions was supposed to unnerve Eric, it was fucking working.

120

"So, I assume you have some questions?" Andy went on. "Save them. Let me put you in the picture with what we know, and then we can talk about why you're here, and how we can help each other out". This was the first sign Eric had received that he wasn't going to end up either in prison or dumped in a well somewhere, and it did help make his heart stop beating like a Phil Collins drum solo.

"You've been busy Mr Curtis, very ingenious to monetise your condition in the way you have"

"Please" he whimpered, "call me Eric". He hated being called by his surname and wanted to give the impression that he was co-operating. Which – when faced with real adversity and being something of an abject coward who would sell his mother to get out of a difficult situation - he was.

"And you can call me Andy. I want to be your friend Eric, I want us to help each other". This guy was good.

"So, this is what we know so far" he started - 'feel free to fill in the blanks if I miss anything. You went to hospital because you ingested some chemicals. You were discharged but not before the chemical experts had taken a good look at you. They suspected Novichok at first, but we put surveillance on you for a bit and after visiting your house a couple of times we realised that your story stacked up and we felt the Russians had more valuable targets to go after than a mid-level call centre manager. As part of our standard protocols, we checked in on you now and again, and our operatives started reporting some odd things happening at your house. Doors opening and closing and no-one going in or out, for example. One of our chaps was at the hospital when you went back to see Doctor..." Barnes paused while his mental rolodex spun round..."Rice, wasn't it? He was there waiting to see a doctor and, busy little bugger that he is, was watching everything. Including doors bursting open and then a man with a crash helmet on wandering about looking lost".

Eric's mind raced back to the waiting room. He could see himself wandering about indoors with his biker gear on and he realised he must have looked very out of place.

Andy Barnes continued: "All this seemed a little odd, so we put you under surveillance. Except we couldn't find you. So we tracked Jane. We saw her going in and out of bookmakers, and we checked what she was betting on, and then what was happening. I'll be honest, it took us a while to figure it out, and even when we did, my boss needed convincing before we moved in"

Eric raised an eyebrow at this which of course, Andy couldn't see but somehow he was able to read his mind.

"Oh yes, everyone has a boss. Mine is the Prime Minister. He's very keen to meet you too. But all in good time"

He went on "so, on a hunch, we got some heat vision goggles on you and you lit up like a bloody Christmas tree. Then everything fell into place. We finally got you at the golf tournament - very clever that one. It's been an interesting time for our operatives, watching you for a few weeks, walking around naked all the time. And this morning, we decided to bring you in for a chat. We reckon you have cleared around four hundred thousand, all told".

Then Andy's mask slipped and his face turned staggeringly malevolent. "Of course, that's been gained illegally, not to mention the fact that you've also been going round assaulting people and you - and Jane - will be spending an awfully long time in prison as a result. Oscar and Kate will be placed into care and we'll sell your house to pay your legal fees".

Andy regained his friendly facade. "But we don't want to walk down that path, do we?"

Eric gulped. "but..but..Andy... We were doing it for charity".

"Ah yes". Said Andy. "The women's shelter. Worthwhile cause. Commendable stuff. We've had a look at their bank accounts. Now tell me. You donated ALL of the money to them?

"No", whispered Eric.

"No". Confirmed Andy. "We promised to be honest with each other, remember? If you lie to me again you'll be choosing a very dangerous path for you, Jane and your children". Andy regained his friendly facade. "But again, we don't want to walk down that path, do we?"

Eric shook his head slowly.

"Good man" said Andy, his smile returning. It was unnerving how quickly he could switch between a kindly uncle and a man who'd eat your eyes if you said the wrong thing. "Now, time to tell you why you're here. Cards on the table. That ok?"

"Sure" Eric replied, hearing his own voice tremble as he had a pretty strong feeling this wasn't going to be anything like a happy compromise.

"So. You want to avoid jail, and you want to stop your kids ending up in the system, agreed?" He asked, somewhat rhetorically.

Eric nodded, meekly and whispered a barely audible "yes Andy".

"Ok, there are some bad people out there Eric. And we think you can help us get them off the streets with your unique condition. A man who can't be seen could make things a lot easier than putting hoods on them and throwing them into the back of vans, don't you think?". Eric thought to himself that Andy had a point there.

"So, in return for immunity from prosecution we're asking you to run a couple of errands for us. In and out. Nice and quick. How does that sound?".

"Do we get to keep the money?" Eric blurted. A stupid question and he regretted it immediately. There was no way he was going to say no, but Eric wanted to feel he was at least in partial control. Even though they both knew he wasn't.

"Absolutely" Andy replied. "Immunity in writing, and you can keep everything you've *stolen* up to now". The heavy intonation on the word 'stolen' was obvious to the pair of them.

Eric shrugged. He was bang to rights. "Thank you Andy" he whispered.

Before the words had left Eric's lips, the door opened and two more suits came in, with one of those government red boxes you see the chancellor hold up on budget day. Suit number one opened it up, and wordlessly handed a single page document to Barnes. He placed it on the desk in front of Eric and from nowhere passed Eric a Mont Blanc pen to sign it.

Of course, it was Kenny Sinclair's monogrammed Mont-Blanc pen. Eric took his time reading the document. He had to go back and re-read several lines, but it all seemed clear enough. Do as we say or you're fucked. That was the general gist. The words 'immunity from all prosecution in perpetuity' were the ones that kept drawing his gaze. Eric signed with something of a flourish, making sure his signature was slightly different to his usual one, which he hoped would make it null and void should he break the agreement. Eric then dropped the pen and wiped his hands on his tracksuit pants

"Ok, and let's use your normal signature on this one" said Barnes, removing the old piece of paper and replacing it with an exact, unsigned copy. This guy was clearly much, much smarter than Eric. He signed next to Eric's name using his own pen, and the paper disappeared back into the box.

'No copy for me', Eric noted sadly to himself.

The suits left, and immediately in rushed Jane, Kate and Oscar. Eric burst into tears, hugging Jane and bending down to cuddle his kids. At first, he didn't register that they had never encountered their Dad in this transparent state before, but to their credit, and after some initial hesitation at the sight before them they returned the hugs with interest.

Clearly Barnes's team had spent some time with Eric's family, filling them in on his situation and explaining to the kids what had happened. Thank Christ for that - it certainly saved him a job. Barnes left them alone. He sent in burgers and cold drinks for them all and the heavies bought in some chairs. "I'll be back in an hour" he said and closed the door. The kids dived onto their burgers and noisily slurped their drinks.

Eric used the distraction and walked over to Jane. "What did they tell you?" he asked

Jane looked tired and scared. "They know everything Eric. Everything. They know how you became invisible, they know about the money, the shelter, everything"

"Anything else?" asked Eric

"They say you stole a car and crashed a bus?" Jane asked, disbelievingly.

Eric batted this away. He was in enough trouble as it was. "And what do the kids know?"

"They've been told you're working for the government and helping them with some experiments, and you're very brave. They're actually quite impressed".

Eric looked down at his kids who had stopped eating and were watching their parents with wide eyed anticipation.

Oscar spoke first. Eric steeled himself for questions about his lies, his broken promises and the experiments. The question took everyone by surprise. "Is your poo invisible too?".

Eric was about to answer when Kate piped up. "Have you been walking naked round the house when my friends have been there? Because that would be gross".

Eric answered each question in turn. Kate was sceptical when Eric promised that no, he'd never been in the house when her friends where there but she eventually looked somewhat convinced.

Jane asked the next question: "Can we keep the money?"

The family chatted properly for the first time as a family in months. The kids told Eric how they'd been made to sign the official secrets act, and their Dad was a hero. 'Thanks Andy', he thought. They both said they'd been promised a dream holiday and even newer mobile phones once the latest mission had been completed but they had to promise not to tell anyone or they could be in danger from some bad people.

The hour passed all too quickly. Andy came in and gently ushered the Jane and the kids out. A lady was assigned to take them home and off they went.

Eric had no idea when he would see them again.

Twenty One

"Right Eric, down to business". This was a new Andy Barnes. Not the kind uncle, or the murdering thug, but somewhere in between. "We have a few targets for you to eliminate. We think each one will be harder than the last, but don't worry, we'll give you all the training and support you need".

'Stop the fucking bus' thought Eric. 'Eliminate?'

Again, Andy seemed to read Eric's mind. "Ok, maybe eliminate is too strong a word. Neutralise". He went on. "Each target is a threat to our national security.

We'll share some case files to help you build a profile, but I warn you that some of the information is very upsetting. I'm sure once you know who we're targeting you won't want to wait to get them off the streets". He opened a dossier. On the front were the words:

ERIC CURTIS. TOP SECRET

They were embossed in gold. It didn't look like something they had rattled off on the photocopier in the last hour, so Eric assumed Andy had known he was going to go along with the plan.

"Do I have a code name?" Eric asked

"Yes, we're going to call you Eric" sighed Andy. Eric would have preferred something cool like Mr Pink, but at least he was fairly confident he could remember his own name.

"Right", said Andy. "Let's get on with it then. Here are the details of the first target. He is an American businessman. He's been living and working for a pharmaceutical company in West London for five years. Thirty nine years old, seemingly happily married, two kids, he's enjoyed a successful and somewhat distinguished career and had over the years become one of the most violent and prolific paedophiles in the UK". The last eight words hung in the air.

Eric bristled. He'd already started to think about who he'd be having to target and assumed it would be a terrorist or fraudsters. But this emboldened him immediately.

"Here are a stack of photographs, and some witness statements, parental testimonies and data lifted from his IP address that pin him squarely to the allegations. And here are copies of encrypted messages from his phone and email, including attachments. Take your time and go through them".

It was horrible. Eric couldn't bring himself to look at much of it, and he could feel his anger rising. The girls in the pictures were all between ten and fourteen. All looked terrified. "Enough" Eric said, snapping the file closed when he'd taken no more than a cursory glance at the evidence before him. "What do we do? How do we do it? What do you need?"

"Good man", said Andy, nodding towards a young woman who had just walked into the room. "This is Rachel Thomson". She'll be your liaison officer from now on, reporting to me. She'll give you what you need, including training, operational details and weapons". Rachel Thomson was in her mid-thirties, slim and pretty but had hands of stone and a gaze that could melt steel. "Thomson, take Eric here and get him up to speed. No fuck ups now. I want this bastard dealt with by tomorrow night".

And with that, he turned on his heels and left.

Twenty Two

Rachel took Eric out of the office that had been his home for the best part of the day. A room where he had entered a criminal and left as an asset of His Majesty's Government. A soon to be trained killer. Well, a scared man with a fear of going to jail anyway.

They went down some stairs, across a few corridors and down again into a large basement. Beautifully furnished, with a gym, a small kitchen, an office and a living room, plus a bedroom and a bathroom. "This will be your base for the next week or so" explained Rachel. Your fingerprint will open the doors, there are men stationed outside and you have a driver on call twenty four hours a day. The markings on your belly (Eric hoped she meant stomach, but decided to let it pass) will wash off with the soap that's in the shower. Get yourself cleaned up and we'll have a dry run at the mission".

Eric did as exactly as he was told. He had a shower, using the soap to clear the yellow paint off. He dried, putting the tracksuit pants back on and walked back into the living area. Rachel was waiting for him, flicking through a file which he assumed (correctly, as it turned out) was Eric Curtis's life history. It was disappointingly thin.

"Ok" she said. "Lose the pants". We need to do make this as realistic as possible". Eric dropped his pants. It was cold in the room, so he was glad he was invisible.

"Now. Your target's name is Daniel Spardell. Here's a picture of him. She flicked on the TV and a photo appeared. Eric recognised him from the file he'd seen in Barnes's office. He works in a big office building in Hammersmith. He travels to work by tube, and is rarely alone. For this to work, he has to be on his own or it will be impossible to pull off in the way we need it to look".

"Why can't you just make him the victim of a violent mugging?" Eric asked.

"Because we want to send a message to the people he interacts with" She replied. Once he's been dispatched, they'll know we're on to them, and hopefully it will scare the shit out of them, knowing they could be next. You're going to poison him, only it will look like a heart attack, and that's how it will be reported. Only his associates will know he's too young and fit to have a heart attack. And we don't want to panic the public with more stories of violent crime"

Rachel took Eric through the plan. They would plant a syringe in the bathrooms of his office building. Eric was to wait for him in one of the stalls, inject him with the syringe while he was taking a dump and leg it, leaving him to be found by a colleague. The autopsy wouldn't note the needle mark in his neck and would duly identify a huge coronary as the cause of death, despite no signs of heart disease. Cameras would show no-one going in or out. No suspect, no murder investigation. The perfect crime.

Rachel showed Eric the syringe and the way to thrust and press in one movement to make sure the contents found their mark. She suggested a live test. Eric laughed. She didn't. She tapped the door which swung open, and in trotted Toto. Of course it would be Toto. The family pet. The kids favourite. Rachel handed him the syringe. "Oh Christ" said Eric. It all suddenly seemed very, very real.

Eric stood up. "No". His voice was firm and strong for the first time that day. "Not Toto". While Toto was undeniably old and putting him out of his misery could have been considered something of an act of kindness, Eric couldn't possibly countenance killing his own dog.

Rachel smiled. "Ok Eric, as you wish". She picked up her phone and started dialling a number into the touch screen. "I had such high hopes for you as well".

Eric was still raging about what Spardell had done to those poor kids. He needed to get this done. The alternative was jail and the breakup of his family. He reached down, scooped Toto up and rammed the needle into his back in one swift movement before allowing himself time to think. Rachel smiled, put down her phone and slowly pulled the syringe out of Toto's back.

"Excellent" she said. "Very impressive"

Toto stared at Eric with barely disguised contempt. His glassy eyes fixing him with a look of hatred and fury.

"How long does it take to work?" Eric asked

"Well, that was only saline solution, so I think he's still got a few years left, judging by the state of him" Rachel laughed.

Eric didn't know whether to laugh or cry. Toto jumped down and padded off to the bedroom and vomited all over the carpet. Staring Eric dead in the eye while he did it. Eric couldn't say he blamed him.

Twenty Three

Rachel walked Eric through the plan. Eric repeated it back to Rachel almost word for word, and then tried to raise a laugh by summarising it: "It sounds like twelve hours of stupefying boredom with sixty seconds of abject panic and confusion. A little like my wedding day". Rachel didn't laugh.

Eric didn't sleep well that night. He wasn't worried about not having the guts to go through with it, He was more afraid of not getting a clean hit and somehow being caught. He imagined Andy Barnes and his team would deny all knowledge of him if that happened, and Eric didn't want to leave his family exposed. At 5am he was up and waiting for the knock on the door. Eric pulled on a soft grey tracksuit and baseball cap, and then Rachel led him to the car park through some narrow corridors and he met the driver, Colin. Eric judged by his haircut and confident gait that Colin was clearly ex-army, and he was so full of wit and wisdom that he helped put Eric's mind at ease. He'd obviously been chosen for that exact purpose, and it relaxed him immediately. Colin greeted Eric with an outstretched hand, not looking in the least surprised that his passenger was missing a face and hands.

Colin was standing next to a black BMW 3 series for this job. Eric said "surely the British taxpayer can do better than this Colin?"

"Helps us blend in laddie" was Colin's answer. "Normally we get Range Rovers or if you're really important, the Bentley, but only when we need to move in a hurry. This is an easy-in, easy-out job. Piece of piss. We're off to West London. Every other car there is a black BMW or Audi.

The traffic on the A4 was very light heading away from the city centre, and soon enough they were easing past a tall office building next to Hammersmith tube station. Colin pulled smoothly into a petrol station next to the building and said: "Ok, off you go pal, leave your tracksuit on the back seat and I'll see you here in twelve hours. Climb over the front and slip out of my door while I'm in the shop buying Jaffa cakes. Oh, and have a nice day now" he cheerily bade Eric farewell and was gone.

Eric stood in the petrol station getting his bearings while just over the road one of the busiest tube stations in London starting hitting rush hour. It suddenly became very real, and for the first time

Eric was having doubts about whether he could do this.

His mind went back to last night's briefing: "the one thing that might happen is you'll freeze and ask yourself if you have the balls to go through with it. That's natural. When it happens, think of Kate and how it could be her in this evil fucker's clutches". It worked. Eric snapped out of his reverie, walked the two hundred yards to the building, dropped under the car park barrier and looked around for the service door.

Getting through the door and finding the stairs was easy enough. Eric jogged up the first flight before realising he'd be the one having the heart attack if he carried on, so slowed down to a lumbering, panting walk for the next seven. He found the eighth floor and slipped through the lobby and into the empty bathroom. The lights flicked on as his presence activated the sensor and he scouted around and found the syringe which had been left, as promised, tucked away on top of the door to trap one. So far, so good. Eric found a small area in the far corner under a sink unit and tried to make himself comfortable. He made sure he could see who was coming in and who was standing at the urinals. It seemed the perfect spot. And then seconds later the door opened.

Andy and Rachel hadn't factored in the cleaner who would come in at 7am with a floor polisher. To be fair, it was the first thing they hadn't planned for, so Eric knew he needed to improvise. Leaping up, he climbed up onto the sink unit and stood, with his arse cheeks pressed against the cold mirror. The cleaner, who Eric thought was probably a minimum-wage Eastern European middle-aged man who was almost certainly over-qualified for this job was extremely thorough. His polisher finding all the dark spaces under the sinks which would certainly have given Eric's balls a nice shine but also blown his cover. He finished cleaning the floor and then started on the mirrors and sinks. 'Ah shit,' thought Eric.

He started at the opposite end of the four sink unit, working towards Eric. He figured he couldn't jump down without making a noise or leaving a footprint on his clean floor, so stood silently to attention and worked out his next move. As the cleaner moved towards Eric he started inching along the mirror to the other end of the sinks. As they crossed, he stopped. Eric's knob was no more than six inches from the cleaner's face. He was staring right at it. Eric's heart was racing. He peered closer. He put his hand up - Eric really thought he was going to cup his balls, but instead, he put his hand to his nose and, holding one nostril closed, blew a mountain of snot out of the other one, all over Eric's right foot which was hovering over the third sink. He turned on a tap and went to grab a cloth to clean what he assumed was the sink when the door swung open, and Daniel Spardell walked in.

As the cleaner turned to see who'd opened the door, Eric stood with his foot under the tap and was able to rinse most of the gunk from his toes in one swift movement. He then hopped to the far sink which had already been cleaned and held his breath.

Spardell stood at the urinal and took a long, loud piss. "The bin in my office needs emptying, my little immigrant friend" he said over his shoulder, in a lazy Southern States drawl, without a hint of irony.

'What a colossal prick', thought Eric.

The cleaner took this as his queue to leave, dragging his equipment with him. Spardell finished his business, zipped up his trousers and walked straight out of the bathroom. "No personal hygiene needed when you molest kids", Eric thought to himself. He exhaled loudly. That hadn't gone to plan at all, and now Eric didn't know when Spardell would be back in the bathroom. He looked like someone who needed a lot of coffee to function, so Eric assumed he would be back soon enough. He crept back under the sink and waited.

Eric had always been great at passing time without feeling bored. He enjoyed his own company and could while away hours in wonderful daydreams. But having no concept of time and lying on a cold, hard fluorescent-lit bathroom floor was different. He ached from the first minute and started to worry He'd cramp up and not be able to move when the time came, so made sure he got up every once in a while and moved around. A dozen or so people came and went, sometimes together, sometimes alone over what felt like the next few hours. Listening to people shitting and blowing noses and taking a piss just a few feet away was fucking awful, and Eric was starting to hope Spardell would come in soon just so he could get away and head back outside.

He came twice more, but was never in the bathroom alone. Eric managed to check someone's watch while he was lying under the sink, it was 3:15pm. He knew his target would be leaving around 5pm so figured he might only have once chance left. He reached and grabbed the syringe from where he'd stashed it, leaving it under a small piece of toilet paper beneath the sink unit so it was close at hand. No sooner had Eric done this than Spardell walked in. Alone.

Rather than head to the urinals, he went into trap two. Eric heard him pull his trousers down. Having listened to people take dumps for eight hours, he knew what to expect. But the sounds of straining and grunting and splashing never came. Instead, the unmistakable sound of a man jerking off. Men know this sound. They try their best to disguise it when their wives are sleeping or when they are in the bath, but all men know what it is. Eric was disgusted - knowing he was probably using the images on his phone or in his head to help him finish. Which he soon enough did, far too noisily for comfort. He flushed, pulled up his trousers, opened the door and then took a syringe full of deadly poison right in his neck. Eric was raging. Before he'd come in and wanked so brazenly in his cubicle of shame, Eric wasn't sure he'd have been able to go through with it but that changed the moment he pulled his pants down and began. He didn't even register Eric was there and went down immediately, banging his head on the toilet as he fell. Eric stood over him for a moment, vile rage and anger coursing through him. Dying like this on a cold bathroom floor was too good for him. Eric considered kicking him in the balls but noticed he had pissed himself. 'Good, that's how he'd be remembered by those who found him and that detail would spread through the office like wildfire' thought Eric. He quickly wrapped the syringe in toilet paper and dropped it in the bin as instructed, and got the fuck out of there.

Eric reversed his earlier journey and found himself sitting in the corner of the petrol station, next to the machine that puts air in car tyres and waited anxiously for Colin. Out of nowhere, and a full two hours early, Colin's BMW appeared. He got out, opened the back door and pretended to look for something, allowing Eric to leap into the car and jump over to the passenger side. Colin closed the back door, glided into the driver's seat and slowly pulled out of the car park, not speaking or glancing towards where Eric was sitting until they were back on the A4. As they eased into the traffic an ambulance siren wailed in the distance, clearly heading in their direction. Eventually, Colin allowed himself a grin and said "How was it mate? All good?". Being the newly trained and qualified, hard-nosed, brutal assassin that Eric was, he burst into tears.

As they approached the MI6 building, Eric regained his composure. Expecting some serious piss-taking from Colin, he was surprised when he gently smiled and said "Happens to us all Eric. The first one is always the hardest. Judging by the welcoming committee, you did great". He nodded ahead, and Eric could see Rachel and Andy standing by the underground car park entrance, beaming smiles on their faces. Colin pulled to a halt and he stepped out. Rachel handed Eric a tracksuit which he hurriedly put on. Eric was getting used to being naked, but it did feel awkward talking to people, knowing they knew you were starkers.

Andy spoke first. "Died instantly, sadly. Cracked his skull on the way down too. Good job. No suspicious circumstances. Next of kin are being informed and our doctor has already issued an interim death certificate. There was a police investigation into him which of course will now be closed. You've saved the taxpayer millions Eric, and spared hundreds of young girls more harm and distress. You're a hero, well done. Now, go and get a good night's sleep. You can take the next few days to recover, get warm and then we'll begin the briefing for target number two. And I don't like to give away too much, but this next one is a whole new level of bastard".

Twenty Four

Eric slept surprisingly well that night. And the night after. The bottle of Jack Daniels and mouthful of Xanax certainly helped. He had room service on demand, but didn't eat much. He figured if he was going to be a government killer he should at least lose a couple of pounds and hit the treadmill with gusto. He'd run a couple of marathons and was still capable of running for thirty minutes without collapsing. Eric asked for some running shoes and kit, and resolved to get as fit as he could, as quickly as he could. Eric wasn't kidding himself that it would make a difference in the next few days, but it helped him focus his mind and gave him somewhere to burn through some adrenalin. As did the training regime.

Eric had been allowed to practice firing some pistols at the underground shooting range, and had been shown some simple self-defence moves to enable him to get out of tight spots. He was keen for them to help him learn some badass punches that would let him drop someone in seconds, but this was apparently "not what we do". Eric really started to miss Jane and the kids, but knew he should just play ball and get this over with as soon as possible.

When Andy came to see Eric almost a week later, he was all business. The jovial man he'd encountered last time they'd met had left the building, and Eric could tell this was serious. "Right Eric, time for your next mission" he snapped. "Your target is overseas. And in twenty four hours, you will be too. I'll give you deniability by not telling you where you will be operating, and the less you know about this one the better, suffice to say he's a very senior member of ISIS and removing him will affect both the operational capability and the financing of this gang of utter bastards"

'Shit' thought Eric. 'Fuck. ISIS. This wasn't some grubby paedo no-one would miss'.

"Thompson will fill you in on the details, but you'll be leaving tonight from RAF Brize Norton, and parachuting in while it's still dark. Good luck, see you in a few days".

"Wait, what? Para-what? Tonight? Brize Norton?" Eric was speechless.

Andy was gone before Eric had a chance to digest the insanity of this. He noted with a pang of despair that this was not even close to being negotiable.

Eric pulled on his faithful tracksuit as Rachel walked in with her dossier.

She sat down and took a deep breath. "Right Eric, here are some of the details. Yes, it is the Middle East. Yes, you'll be parachuting in - although strapped to an SAS soldier, and yes, it would be creeping through the midst of a highly active and very nervous and well-guarded terrorist camp. This time, there will be nowhere to store the syringe near the target".

"Why on earth not?" asked Eric. "I thought you lot could do anything"

Rachel said "actually we didn't know where the target was until this morning. We can't leave syringes with poison all over the desert just in case a terrorist happens to set up camp nearby"

Eric hadn't thought of that. "so I guess I have to beat him to death with my bare hands then? Why can't you take him out with a drone strike".

"We need to be absolutely sure we get him" explained Rachel. "Despite what you might see on TV with laser guided bombs dropping down chimneys, we never quite know when we've been successful. We need you to ID him and ensure he's dead. It's vital that we get a positive result on this one. Too many people have died and even more are at risk because of this guy".

Colin arrived to take them to the RAF base. This time, he had the Range Rover although it didn't make the ride any more comfortable. Eric sat in silence, his mind racing and wondering if life in prison wouldn't be preferable to all this madness. He felt his heart pounding and beads of sweat had started to form on his back at the very thought of the next few days. Rachel sensed this and turned to him. "Eric, relax. I know it seems difficult, but it always does until it's done. The Hammersmith operation went beautifully, you're a natural".

Eric felt anything but a natural. He felt like a total imposter.

Rachel continued by pulling out a mini syringe and a tub of Vaseline. "Look, you can either carry this in your hand or hide it somewhere. It's up to you".

"Thanks Rachel. The option of shoving a highly deadly poison attached to a razor sharp needle up my arse is really helping to set my mind at ease." Rachel laughed at this.

"Ok, carry it then", she said. "I have every confidence in you".

Colin weaved through the traffic heading west, passing Eric's Porsche dealership. The blue 911 had gone and had been replaced by one of their large family station wagons which was a dull grey and looked nauseatingly uninspiring. Eric remembered that was the day before he'd been picked up by the government and suddenly wished he was simply stealing cars and fleecing bookmakers rather than doing shit like this. He wasn't James Bond or Jason Bourne. He wasn't even Justin Bieber. What on earth was happening?

Suddenly, Eric yearned for his former boring, mundane life. While he found the opportunity to serve his country genuinely exciting, He was hopelessly out of his depth and totally ill-prepared to do what was being asked of him. But he had no choice. If he didn't, the only place he'd be going, along with Jane, was behind bars.

Twenty Five

As they boarded the giant C-130 Eric felt like making a run for it. Sensing his nerves, Colin gripped Eric's shoulder. "This fucker is planning something big mate, bigger than 9/11. Do the world a favour and wipe him out for us". Eric's resolve suitably stiffened, he climbed up the ramp at the back of the plane and plonked himself down in a hard metal seat and fastened his seat belt. Colin wished Eric good luck, saluted Rachel and then marched back to the Range Rover. His tail lights disappeared from view and Eric gulped.

The flight was noisy and bumpy, but Rachel pulled on some headphones and gestured for Eric to do the same.

"Ok Eric, here we go". She opened a file which included a series of maps and diagrams. "I'll be using hand gestures and diagrams and you need to remember this stuff, so pay attention".

Hand gestures and maps didn't feel like they covered all the requisite bases for this evening's entertainment but Eric was way past the point of complaining and had no alternative plan to offer, so he shut up and paid attention.

Soon, Rachel was shouting into her microphone to be heard over the plane's engines, she began the briefing: "We'll be landing at an Afghan army base here and picking up a helicopter and your parachute buddy. We'll climb above the surface to air missiles and drop in exactly 3kms from the camp. You'll be walking dead North until you find the base".

"How will I know which way North is?" asked Eric

"Your guide will point you in the right direction. All you have to do is walk in a straight line. Think you can manage that?". This sounded sarcastic and

Rachel immediately put her hand up to apologise. "Don't worry Eric, we'll show you where to go. Now, here is a picture of your target. He should be easy enough to identify. We know that as of yesterday he is clean shaven, and has short hair, he wears John Lennon wire-rimmed glasses but is fat and short. He'll probably be sleeping so you'll need to sneak around, find his tent, pump him full of lethal drugs and walk back the three kilometres in the dark. Just make sure you are heading dead South, where you'll be met by a friendly British soldier who'll get you back to the extraction point and we'll be home in time for tea and medals". She smiled to confirm the ease of the plan. Eric wasn't smiling.

Several uncomfortable, noisy and cold hours later, they were landing. Eric wasn't told where they were, but it was a huge army base with American and British soldiers and equipment everywhere. Rachel told him to put on fatigues, gloves and a balaclava and goggles. Eric suggested it would be less conspicuous if he were invisible although as he stepped off the plane there were at least three dozen men dressed exactly like him. No-one gave the pair a second glance, and with Rachel also dressed in fatigues they slipped through the base effectively unnoticed. Rachel seemed to know exactly where they were headed and they zigzagged between semi-permanent tents until they found an anonymous looking building near the centre of the base. She pulled the door opened and nodded for Eric to head inside.

The room was brightly lit, and filled with the smell of testosterone, cigarettes and coffee. There were four men playing cards on a couple of smart looking sofas who immediately stood to attention as the pair entered. Rachel saluted, and said "at ease men".

Eric turned to face her, startled and thought to himself. 'Who the fuck was this woman?'

Rachel introduced Eric to each man in turn, at which point he realised he still had his mask and goggles on. Eric went to take them off and Rachel immediately stopped him. "Not yet Eric", she said. She asked three of the men to leave, with just Rachel, Eric and the smallest of the soldiers left in the room. "Eric, meet Will. He's going to be helping you fall out of a helicopter in about two hours time. And he knows, so you can de-mask now". Eric pulled off his gloves and mask and went to shake Will by the hand. He stood, opened mouthed, not returning the offered hand, which Eric realised he couldn't see.

"Sorry, I don't mean to stare", said Will, "but fuck me, that is some freaky shit".

"None taken" Eric laughed

A grin appeared on Will's face. "I've seen some stuff mate, but this takes the fucking digestive, I must say. I heard about you at the briefing but thought it was a wind up, that is until Major Thomson here rocked up now"

Major Thomson? Wow. Eric didn't know much about army ranks but knew Major was one of the people who didn't generally get shot at on the battlefield. He thought about the call centre world and how it was famously hung up on job titles, with a Head of Operations generally being the big Kahuna. Once again, he realised how totally inconsequential his life had been to that point, and how much he'd missed by spending years on such a futile activity.

Rachel went through the plan again, this time without the overbearing competition of the sound of huge engines. Will seemed fabulously at ease with it all. "I'll try not to get an erection on the way down mate, don't worry" he laughed. "I don't want you falling in love with me". That was, by some distance, the least of Eric's worries but again, his confidence and positivity was infectious. He went on

"I'll be keeping half an eye on you. If you aren't back in two hours I'll call in a drone strike, so just make sure you're out of the way if that happens. And I'll point you in the right direction when we land, so you don't go galloping off into the night towards Kabul".

"Excellent" said Eric. "That would be appreciated".

Soon enough, Eric and Will were up in the chopper. It was smaller than he'd imagined with just four seats and remarkably quiet compared to the C-130. The pilot had the windows open and Eric could hear him and the base chatting in the headphones using that weird pilot / control tower language that seems so alien. Within a few minutes the chatter stopped just leaving the rhythmic thudding of the rotors above. Eric tried to crack a joke about turning the big fan off but Will put his finger to his lips and mouthed the words 'enemy territory'. It suddenly felt very, very real, and very, very scary. Eric had seen enough movies to know the hills and valleys below almost certainly contained a load of bad guys with rocket launchers and they were scanning the sky, just waiting for some target practice. At once, the noise of the rotor blades seemed to increase tenfold and Eric was convinced they were about to be shot down. He gripped Will's arm, desperate for some reassurance. Will patted his hand. "You'll be fine mate, I promise".

Eric took a deep breath and started to pull his fatigues off when Will stopped him. "If they can see me as we land, you're fucked anyway, so rather keep warm until we hit the deck. And put these goggles on, you'll need them. I'll keep your clothes with me until you get back and we can get you all dressed up for dinner as we head back, ok?" That was just fine with Eric.

Will put on his chute, stood up and beckoned Eric over before strapping him in like a small baby kangaroo to its mother's pouch, fixing an oxygen mask over his mouth. The light turned green and without any warning they were suddenly outside, hurtling through the air. The noise was initially deafening and Eric put his hands instinctively over his ears. Will appeared in total control, pointing them towards the ground and using his watch to locate the landing zone. He pulled the chute and everything went blissfully quiet as they floated towards the ground and landed with a gentle thump, Will rolling on top of Eric and popping up while releasing both harnesses and folding his parachute in one single, impressive movement before whipping both their masks off. "Right, keep quiet, whispers only and I'll be using sign language from now on, ok?". Eric did exactly as he was told.

Eric quickly disrobed and let his eyes adjust to the night sky. The ground was mainly hard rock and sand, with small jagged stones littering the floor and soon enough he was angrily rubbing pebbles from the soles of his feet. Will gripped Eric's shoulders, pointed to a bright star in the distance and held up three fingers. He then pointed to an even brighter star in the opposite direction and then at himself. Right, those were the North and South markers. Eric studied them both carefully, and nodded, again, forgetting Will couldn't see him. He whispered "got it". Will whispered back "right, now fuck off". Eric was about to pop the greased syringe into place when he realised he didn't need to until he was near the camp. It was very dark and he could barely see three yards in front of his face so figured it unlikely that anyone would spot a three inch syringe floating along in the darkness.

Eric counted his steps as he jogged through the dessert, clutching the syringe and glancing up into the night sky at the Northern star while cursing every stone that embedded itself painfully into the soles of his feet. He knew from his marathon days that his running gait was about 1 metre a step, so figured he should be tripping over the camp at roughly three thousand steps. Counting as he ran helped with the abject panic he was feeling and he focused on that rather than what was about to happen. He kept glancing up at the sky, tracking his star and making sure he was heading in the right direction. Amazingly, Eric was bang on - the sound and smells of a crackling campfire coming into his senses at step 2,750.

Eric slowed to a walk, and then an ultra-cautious tip-toe. The camp soon came into view. It was much smaller than he'd imagined. Half a dozen canvas tents, and a single guard, who looked asleep by the fire. Again, Eric debated sticking the needle up his backside then made the executive decision that still no-one could see it anyway, so thought he'd chance it. He circled the camp once as instructed, casing the area out and making sure there were no guards peeing in bushes or patrolling the perimeter before arriving back at his entry point and taking stock of the situation.

Eric picked the biggest tent first and slipped through the flap. It was pitch dark. He couldn't see anything. John Lennon himself could have been in there singing 'Twist and Shout' and he wouldn't have spotted him. Fuck.

Eric tried a couple more tents. The same thing - all in darkness. Just the sound of snoring and the stench of shit coffee and bad breath. Bollocks. He knew he had about forty minutes before he had to head back. He needed to think of something.

He crept towards the fire and considered his options. Grabbing a large, burning branch, Eric flicked it towards the single guard. It landed squarely in his lap, and this led him, somewhat unsurprisingly, to awake from his doze and have something of a meltdown. He started screaming and panicking. Eric didn't profess to know any Arabic, but he suddenly heard the direct translation of "get this fucking burning log off me".

It was at this point that gas lights began flicking on and tent flaps started being flung open and bleary-eyed soldiers wandered into the clearing to see what the commotion was all about. Most were soon laughing at their colleague's predicament and there was typical piss-taking with no real offers of help. And that's when Eric saw the target. He was wearing Mickey Mouse boxer shorts and the unmistakable John Lennon glasses. Eric whipped across from his spot by the fire and had the syringe in his throat and the contents in his blood stream before you could say "come on, Pluto". He crashed to the ground and Eric was off, sprinting away from the camp, tossing the syringe into the fire as he went. He had covered around a quarter of a kilometre before pausing and listening for sounds of being followed.

The camp had exploded into noise and lights and torches swept the landscape around Eric. The night air was filled with the sound of murderous terrorists - seemingly yelling about the audacity of someone killing one of their leaders in cold blood but Eric was confident no-one was following him.

He gathered his breath and looked up for the tell-tale star. When he was with Will, it was very easy to spot. Almost obvious. Actually harder to miss. Now they all looked the same. He stared intently at the sky, hoping that one of them would leap out of the cluster of thousands he could see and point the way to his ride home, but the more he stared, the more they all looked identical.

Eric shivered in the cold and the goosebumps that covered him were part temperature, and part abject panic. The voices were undoubtedly getting closer, and the arc of torchlight was only a few hundred metres away and closing. Eric was deep inside a foreign country, being hunted by killers with a score to settle, with temperatures dropping and fuck knows what crawling around ready to bite him on the balls. He wasn't even sure which country he was in, and even if he knew, he wasn't smart enough to figure out which way was North, let alone which country was North of the country he didn't know he was in. 'Think Eric, think' he began to tell himself.

Eric retraced his steps to the camp, hoping he could work out which way he'd come in, with a plan forming in his maelstrom mind of sprinting off back in the direction he'd arrived from. The bad guys were going bananas. They were still running around, looking for the deadly assassin who'd killed their glorious leader. He was lying, face down by his tent. Eric don't know if they assumed he'd been hit by a sniper, but they were waving guns around and yelling at each other in very angry voices.

After a few minutes of increasing panic, Eric found his original entry point and looked up - picked the brightest star he could see and started to run. The stony ground continued to hurt his feet like a bastard, but adrenalin pushed him on, again counting the steps as he went. He got to 1500 when he felt a "whoosh" pass overhead - Will had clearly assumed the worst and called in the drone. Eric turned to follow its path and stood open-mouthed as a couple of dozen of the world's most evil bastards simply ceased to exist. The light burned into Eric's retinas and he was rocked backwards, but his mind stayed alert and he knew he had to get back to Will before the helicopter came to whisk him, minus Eric, out of this shit storm.

Eric ran the next 1400 steps or so as fast as he could, no longer caring that he was panting and kicking up dust and hardly inconspicuous. Out of the darkness a small flashlight appeared, blinking twice. As he sprinted towards Will a helicopter came out of nowhere and they bundled aboard. Will blindly held out a pair of headphones and Eric quickly put them on.

"Never in doubt mate, I knew you'd do it" he beamed. "The drone was an insurance policy, I was sure you were on your way back". Eric was still panting from his run, and pulling on army fatigues and rubbing stones from the soles of his feet. When he could speak, he filled Will in on the evening's fun and games. He finished the story as they started to descend. Will said nothing, just gave Eric a manly punch on the shoulder and grunted "top job mate, top job".

Rachel met the pair from the helicopter with a salute and a handshake. "Time for a celebratory drink" she smiled. Eric could tell the mood in the entire camp had lifted. News had filtered through the different squadrons and he could hear music and laughter where before it had been notably quiet and subdued. As they headed to the tent a few soldiers we passed saluted Rachel and offered her a 'well done Ma'am'. Eric didn't think it appropriate to point out who the real hero of the hour was in case she beat the shit out of him.

They sat in the mess, watching the rolling news reporting a "major victory in the war on terror". It was an odd experience, the three of them, whiskey in hand, listening to the breathless reporting of what they'd done only an hour ago. Obviously the army had fed the story to the press to help win the information war, and pictures of the (now dead) ISIS leader were being beamed around the world with a red cross covering his grinning face. The reporter spoke of a special operation, undertaken by Britain's most skilled and brave soldiers. Will spluttered on his drink. "Undertaken by a naked twat who doesn't know which way South is, more like".

It was hard for Eric to argue with that.

Twenty Six

Twelve hours later, Eric was back in the basement which had become his second home. He had taken to wearing a baggy khaki tracksuit, beanie and glasses to give himself something of a human appearance. Oscar, Kate and Jane were there to greet him. They never even considered discussing where their Dad been or what he'd done, and the kids didn't care anyway. They just knew their Dad was helping the government out and that was good enough for them. They had a great day with as much takeaway, ice-cream and fizzy drinks as they could manage and Jane and Eric even managed some time to just cuddle on the couch watching telly while the kids played on their phones. Eric looked around at his family. The overwhelming sense of love he had for them flooded his senses and he squeezed Jane tightly.

Eric was emotionally knackered and ready for bed when there was a knock on the door. Rachel came in without being asked, followed by Andy and the unmistakable figure of the Prime Minister. Oscar and Kate didn't have a clue who he was so hardly raised an eyebrow, until Jane demanded that they get up and shake his hand.

The PM had a booming voice and a charismatic presence. "Your Dad is a bloody hero, you should be incredibly proud of him".

Both children looked towards Eric with quizzical expressions so he replied "clearly our PM is an intelligent and astute judge of character, and you should vote for him forever" which got a hearty laugh and a huge slap on the back.

Andy spoke next. "Eric, the Prime Minister. Prime Minister, Eric".

Eric offered an outstretched sleeve. The PM shook it vigorously. "A pleasure to meet you sir" he said. "Barnes here has told me about your adventures and we're all jolly proud of you". Until then, Eric had assumed the PM's posh public school accent was a shtick that he used for the benefit of his party faithful, but it was obvious that's how he spoke.

Andy intervened. "Right Eric, we think you've earned a holiday. There is more to be done, but you'll need a full debrief and a couple of weeks off after your efforts last night. Rachel will sort out the details".

He turned to leave, but before he did the PM pulled Eric conspiratorially to one side and whispered in his ear: "Eric, your next mission will be more political in nature. I'll consider it a personal favour if you agree to it, however I warn you it will seem like an odd request. I'll be in your debt if you pull it off and will find a way to repay you if it all works out". He tapped his nose, gave Eric an unnerving wink and was gone.

Rachel interrupted the silence. "Hey kids, how would you like a special treat".

"Yes" they screamed in unison, and Colin appeared out of nowhere, swinging his car keys. "Who wants a trip to the biggest computer shop in London?" He asked.

Eric was grateful - some more alone time with Jane would be welcome but secretly he was a little jealous that they children were being taken away for a few hours. He had really started to enjoy their company and the connections the family were finally making. Eric reached for his wallet when Rachel stopped him. "His Majesty's Government will cover the cost Eric, it's the least we can do".

The kids turned to Jane, wide-eyed, begging for approval. Jane suggested jokingly that this was a way to get them off our hands for a couple of hours so happily agreed. Eric suddenly realised Jane had effectively been a single mum for the past few weeks and also needed a break. They practically bowled Colin over as they ran for the car park and suddenly it was just the three of them.

Rachel poured more drinks. Eric had already planned to drink lots of whiskey that night and party into the early hours like he used to. He'd really cut down on the alcohol in the last month or so but was still more than capable of jumping back into that pond, but a new feeling was taking over. Dad, husband, self. For a long time it had been the other way round, and Eric felt a glow he hadn't felt in years. As he sipped a glorious single malt that tasted like honey, he raised a quiet glass to relief, to excitement, to adventure and because he felt like a hero that could achieve anything. Most of all he felt like a good person doing good things. He started to think of the future. Of a life with his family, doing mundane things he's have considered boring just a few short months ago. He thought of these things as he passed out twenty minutes later on the couch.

Early the next morning, Eric woke with a start. "Take cover!" he screamed, the image of a drone flying over his head and the bright light burning a hole in his memory. The kids rushed in to see their mum holding their dad tightly. She motioned for them to come and join the family hug. Eric felt instantly calmed. "sorry", he mumbled, "bad dream, that's all".

He wandered into the kitchen and expected to see empty bottles and beer cans littered around the counter tops like the old days, but only spied the single malt and a gin bottle, both with only a few measures missing. He opened the fridge to see an unopened twelve pack of his favourite beer. 'Jesus

Eric, you're getting old' he whispered to himself, smiling broadly as he closed the fridge.

He was relieved to discover no hangover, but as the kids had bought themselves a laptop each and an Xbox and a Bluetooth speaker the noise was just beyond bearable he suggested unplugging them all to get some quiet. The emptiness filled the room, so Eric said "No, bugger it, noise is good, crack on kids".

Rachel suddenly appeared through the front door. "Colin will be here in an hour to pick you all up, see you when you get back. Don't worry about packing, it's all been done for you". She shook Eric's hand, walked over the Jane and the kids and hugged them all tightly. "Thanks for lending us your Dad" she said.

Twenty Seven

Colin appeared exactly an hour later, scooped them all up in a seven seater Land Rover and drove them to Brize Norton. The King's RAF jet was standing by and they were soon on their way to the Turks and Caicos Islands. Andy had organised a private secluded villa where the family spent the next two weeks sitting on the beach, having picnics and listening to music, water-skiing and snorkelling. The nearest neighbouring villa was over a mile away, and the white sandy beaches, azure blue waters and endless sunshine was the perfect post-terrorist assassination tonic.

Andy had laid on a chef and a retinue of cleaners who seemed to always work when they weren't around. The villa was always scrubbed and tidied overnight, the fridge restocked and they never saw another soul. The whole family went deep-sea fishing, they barbecued their catch and sat around the fire as the sun went down and bonded like never before. Eric had finally stopped seeing the flash of the missile in his head as he closed his eyes and was getting some sleep again. With his family around, a clear head and blue skies he was refreshed, re-energized and happy.

Having no mission to worry about, and endless hours sitting on a sun lounger while waves gently lapped the white sandy beach, Eric was able to spend some time reflecting on being invisible, and considered some of the realities of his condition.

On the negative side, he had to be totally naked in order to not be seen. This meant his feet hurt from walking outdoors, so he was cold and miserable unless it was sunny, he couldn't carry anything, especially a phone which meant there was no way to navigate or communicate once he was out of reach. He had to be ultra-careful not to leave footprints or make a noise when around people. The biggest drawback was now how he couldn't just go out with the kids and Jane and do things a normal family would do. Of course he could be there, but family photos of holidays and days out would look a little odd. Eric avoided crowds so people didn't bump into him and he did wonder what would happen if he ever broke a bone or became ill. He reflected on his time trying to even see Doctor Rice back when all this started and how he was dismissed out of hand. Eric supposed the government would have someone they could refer him to, but then he counted the number of people who even knew he existed in this state. Not including the soldiers who'd kidnapped him, there was the PM, Andy Barnes, Will, Colin and Rachel Thomson. He suddenly realised he was still quite deniable.

But of course there were plusses. They had £300k sitting untouched in a watering can in a shed in Berkshire. he could go anywhere, do anything and watch any sporting or music event or even a movie for free if he chose to do so. He hadn't done this yet but resolved to make sure he checked for any impending good concert dates when he got home. He felt like he was working for the good guys too. Andy had told Eric that the terrorist network had been badly damaged by the death of the ISIS leader and he was riding his motorbike every day. And the family. Everything went back to the family. They were closer than ever, but he still felt he couldn't fully use this rekindled love for them while in this state. As he reflected, he suddenly felt melancholic. He really wanted his old life back. The one he had been so bored with previously.

Twenty Eight

Two weeks later and the kids were back at school. Jane was depositing their cash into a government-approved bank account, and Eric was in the Prime Minister's office, "showing off his tan". A joke the PM laughed at a little too long for Eric's liking.

"Now Eric, remember that personal favour you promised to do for me?". Of course, he promised no such thing, but he let him carry on. "You'll baulk when I tell you this, but I need you to hear me out". While he was confident the Eric vs Country slate was beginning to be wiped clean, he was also starting to enjoy the work. Eric had no idea how long he would be needed for, and naively assumed that two major bad guys taken care of had gone a long way to levelling the ledger. He made a mental note to ask Andy next time he saw him.

Eric nodded. "What do you need big man?". He hated this expression as soon as it came out his mouth and the Prime Minister visibly baulked at the jarring words.

"Call me Prime Minister. You seem like a decent guy Eric. Don't get an ego, It'll get you killed. Your man Will told me that, and he seems like he knows what's what". Fair enough.

"So, the mission. You know my nemesis...?" The Prime Minister stopped and took a slurp of tea. They both knew exactly who he was referring to. "Well, he's speaking at a conference in a few days and I think we need to make an exhibition of him, don't you?"

No, Eric did not think that. He didn't think that at all. "Umm, not really Prime Minister. "I'm not sure I follow, and I'm not sure this is something I can help you with. I think you may need to consider someone else for this. I have morals, you know".

Which is why, a few days later, Eric found himself at a conference centre in Brighton where the leader of the opposition would be attacking the Government for being duplicitous and evil. Eric was now on the Ministry of Defence payroll, being paid quite a lot of money for his services. Morals have a price, and that price was a six figure salary, free holidays, zero income tax and not going to jail.

Eric had been flown down to the coast on a navy helicopter, all dressed up in a flying suit with helmet, goggles and sunglasses. They landed at the Quebec barracks and he hopped down from the chopper and walked to the main building as instructed.

He swapped the helmet for a cap and oversized sunglasses and walked through to the main road, and as promised, a smart BMW with tinted windows sat waiting. Eric opened the door and climbed into the back, quickly undressing as the silent driver sped them through the city and towards the venue which even from a distance looked busy with delegates and reporters milling about outside.

They pulled into a bus stop about half a mile from the conference hall which was about as close as the police cordon would allow. Eric opened the door and eased out of the car, keeping his distance from the crowds and walking towards the large building. Soon enough, he found a back door to the hall where he could sneak past the guards and make his way inside. The back door led to some wide corridors and he kept tight to the walls to avoid bumping into anyone before finding the auditorium and making his way to the side of the stage.

The conference hall was already full and there was a buzz of anticipation as the delegates waited for what the Prime Minister had called their vainglorious, pontificating leader to take to the stage. Eric wasn't particularly political. He voted on local issues. Who'd get the bins collected, who'd keep the schools in books and pens - that kind of thing, and didn't pay much heed to national or international affairs, but he knew this guy and he did seem extremely zealous to Eric. So left wing he was almost right wing, carrying a cult of personality around him. Promising to renationalise everything, double taxes for everyone except his core voters and lock up anyone who voiced a dissenting opinion to all this on social media. Eric had been assured this would lead to hyperinflation, a housing crash and a crippling recession, but that hadn't really been the driving influence to him agreeing to this plan. That was still very much the threat of prison and the need to keep Andy and his boss happy.

The PM had promised the drops of liquid Eric was giving him wouldn't cause lasting damage, but would rather "incapacitate" him for a month. Two, tops. Not asking any questions, and therefore being told no lies, he had agreed. He'd be saving democracy, he was told. Eric actually believed it too. Almost.

The stage crew were milling around, running their final sound checks and making sure the teleprompter was working ok. Eric felt for the seam in the curtain and found what he was looking for quickly enough. Exactly as promised, a small bottle had been sewn into the material and he was able to prise it loose and scoop it up in his fist. Eric leopard crawled over the stage, clutching the small vial of clear liquid in his hand. It was small enough to be unnoticeable and seconds later he was standing at the podium, carefully dropping the clear, syrupy liquid into the filled glass of water that had been positioned for the leader. Eric scooted to the back of the stage. All doors and exits were now closed, so he figured he should simply wait it out with a superb view of the frivolities and slip out once the commotion started.

A full twenty minutes later than planned, he walked out. No tie, hand-made bespoke designer suit crumpled just enough to give off a "man of the people vibe" and a shit-eating grin that made Eric suddenly feel nothing but disgust for this prick. That might have just been him trying to make himself feel better, and it worked. The leader stalked the front of the stage, soaking up the adulation from (again, the Prime Minister's words rang in Eric's ears) 'the great unwashed, unemployed and socially retarded tossers who'd come to pray at his altar'.

Finally, after a few minutes of his name being chanted and general adulation, he positioned himself at the podium. He stood next to it, leaning against it with his elbow. He reached for the water, took a big swig, and began his speech.

"COMRADES", he yelled. The crowd went wild. "This corrupt, incompetent government...." he stopped. He dropped the glass, its remaining contents spilling into the carpet. He doubled over in pain. He groaned. Eric couldn't see his face but could tell he was in big trouble. Whatever was in that vial worked fast. He lifted his head and projectile vomited over some of the shadow cabinet in the front two rows. Eric didn't believe you could have such projection when being sick but apparently he was wrong. It was barrelling out of his throat like a hosepipe, as he turned it missed Eric by inches. That felt like his cue to leave. Mayhem broke out in the hall. Medics raced to the stricken MP's aid, those caught in the front row crossfire raced to the bathrooms or back to their hotels (for what Eric assumed would be quite a long shower and a burning of their clothes) and he slipped out behind the stage and through an emergency exit which had been pushed open by a retching shadow minister.

There was panic in the hall with shrieks and screams from delegates and security staff alike and paramedics raced past Eric with a look of genuine alarm on their faces. The room was illuminated with the flashes from dozens of press photographers taking the pictures that would be all over the front pages of tomorrow's newspapers, and the sound of reporters breathlessly narrating into the banks of television cameras the gory details of what they had just witnessed. Eric was no political expert, but even he knew this wouldn't play well with the electorate.

He made his escape and was back in the staff car and then spirited away on the helicopter within minutes and heading back to London and the Ministry of Defence building. The Prime Minister was waiting for him. "Bloody good show Eric" he boomed. "Top stuff. Hilarious. The media are already suggesting he doesn't have the stomach for the fight. Stomach, do you get it?".

No, the British press's sense of humour was too nuanced, Eric thought.

"Right, I owe you one. Whenever you need a favour, give me a call". He scribbled his personal number on a piece of paper and left, chuckling at the brilliance of his plan.

The media were utterly ruthless. The emergency services had taken the MP to hospital and despite not saying what he was suffering from, the insinuation was that drink was involved and perhaps something stronger to help him "concentrate". Politically, he was finished and he announced his resignation from his very expensive, non-state funded private hospital room a few days later due to "ill health". It turned out he had a drink and substance abuse problem after all, and by his own admission, wasn't strong enough to be Prime Minister.

The Prime Minister insisted Jane and Eric join him for dinner in Downing Street that evening to say thank you properly. Jane was waiting for her husband in his quarters, already dressed in her finest evening wear. She'd bought Eric his one good suit from home and he was pleased to note it was a little loose around the waist which showed what laying off the beer and crisps could do.

They were driven into Downing Street and secreted in via the private rear entrance, ready for their state banquet, only to be greeted by the Prime Minister and his wife in matching khaki tracksuits. He had wanted to make the Curtises feel comfortable and didn't think to confirm the dress code. Even so, they had a great evening and he was spectacularly indiscreet, telling them who of his cabinet colleagues were useless (all of them), which ones were having affairs (all of them) and which ones were plotting to take his job (all of them). He served a huge roast turkey but had convinced Jane it was actually swan, as that's the only thing Prime Ministers are allowed to eat when entertaining guests. He always came across as a bit of a pompous twat on television, but in an informal setting was huge fun to be around. As they left for the night he gave Eric huge bear hug and reminded him to call him if he ever needed his help.

Twenty Nine

Andy called Eric the following morning and told him that he wouldn't be needed for at least a week. Eric asked if he could use the week to visit the United States, and in particular Nevada and the Grand Canyon. Eric explained to Andy that spending some time driving through the great American heartland had always been on his and Jane's bucket list and this would fulfil a lifelong ambition of theirs, as well as allowing him to spend some time alone with his wife for the first time in ages. Surprisingly, he was told that it would be fine. They could hire an RV with a warning to "be bloody careful". The kids were duly packed off to their aunt and a few days later the Curtises were flown over on a government jet to Las Vegas, where a shiny motorhome was parked and fuelled for them. Jane took the wheel and they were off, picking their way through the airport, out past the famous 'Welcome to Las Vegas' sign, past Chinatown and then onto the I95 heading North West. Eric wasn't planning on touring too many roads or landmarks, he knew exactly what he wanted to check out for himself.

Eric wasn't a conspiracy theorist at all, but a few moments in history had always intrigued him. Who really killed JFK? Did man really land on the moon? Why did the BBC keep commissioning Mrs Brown's Boys? He'd been thinking about these things, and many others, and wondering if there was a way he could find the answer to something really big and interesting. He had no intention of doing anything with the information if he found out, but he figured if he could peak behind the curtain of something remarkable, why wouldn't he? Eric really wanted to be able to whisper something suitably interesting on his death bed that would mess with people's minds after he was gone. He hadn't used his invisibility for anything other than stealing, settling scores or doing the government's bidding. This was something he wanted to do just for himself.

Area 51 is about an hour's drive out of Vegas, and although he was pretty sure Andy and his team would be tracking them, he figured by the time they knew where they were heading there wouldn't be much they could do to stop them. Jane drove sensibly, keeping just below the speed limit and soon enough they reached the outskirts of the famous military base which was built in the middle of the desert and had long been rumoured to house alien craft that had landed near Roswell in 1947. Eric didn't believe in little green men but he was curious to know if the truth really was out there. He wanted to believe.

The motorhome cruised through the desert, gliding slowly past the northern side of the base as Jane looked for somewhere to pull over without drawing the attention of the American authorities who would undoubtedly be watching with interest.

Jane and Eric's phones suddenly rang simultaneously. A withheld number. They exchanged nervous glances.

"Don't answer it" said Eric. "That's Andy, somehow calling us both at exactly the same time, and he'll be calling to ask what exactly the fuck we think we are doing, and to abort, abort, abort".

"Well what ARE we doing Eric?" asked Jane. She still believed they were sightseeing. Eric wanted her to have absolute deniability so hadn't let her in on his plan. He was not sure she'd have gone along with this insanity if he'd told her. She suddenly didn't look particularly happy.

"Please tell me you aren't going to do what I think you're going to do?" She asked, although it was more of a warning than a question.

"Oh come on. It'll be fun. You head off for a shopping spree somewhere, and pop back here at 6pm. I'll jump in and tell you exactly what's inside. Don't pretend you don't want to know. We used to watch the X-Files when were first dating. I'll be careful. Turn both phones off, stick them in the glove box and I'll see you tonight". And without giving Jane time to tell him he was a total arsehole, Eric was out the door and into the desert.

It was blisteringly hot, and Eric was only wearing a pair of shorts, t-shirt and flip flops. He undressed, keeping just the sandals on as the ground looked very stony as he figured his choice of footwear wouldn't be noticed, and he could step out of them when he'd worked out his plan of entry.

Jane pulled away and carried on up the road. Eric didn't know if she'd be back at the same spot at 6pm, she seemed pretty pissed off. He figured that was future Eric's problem.

He watched her drive into the distance until she was a tiny speck, the settling clouds of dust were the only sign anyone had been on the deserted highway. She disappeared over the horizon and Eric suddenly felt very alone. They had been true partners in crime over the recent months and he wanted to share the fun stuff with her. But here in heavily militarized zone she'd surely be shot on sight if she wandered into the base, so she'd have to make do with a day of browsing the malls while Eric went off like a giddy schoolboy on what she would later almost certainly call a 'bloody stupid adventure'.

Eric started to walk along the fence on the north side and spotted a security gate about a mile from where he was dropped. The ground was by now largely hard sand, so he slipped out of the flip flops and headed as quietly as he could towards it. He checked he wasn't leaving footprints, and although it was very warm he wasn't leaving sweat stains on the ground either. All good. He could feel beads of perspiration on his forehead but they were evaporating before they hit the ground. Eric imagined any t-shirt he'd have been wearing would have been soaked through by now. He was also grateful he couldn't get sunburnt, although Jane had managed to convince him to cover up with factor fifty during the first days of their beach holiday but they soon discovered it made him very visible and was very difficult to wash off.

About a hundred yards from the gate Eric started to notice the surveillance cameras everywhere, and a couple of soldiers in the air-conditioned little security hut. The boom gate was blocking the vehicular entrance, and he squatted down and half crawled, half walked underneath it, watching the guards the whole time. They didn't give any indication of noticing him so he pushed on. The rattling hum of the air conditioning units provided enough background noise to protect the sound of his quiet footsteps. The main building was dead ahead of him, but still some distance away. Eric figured it was a mile and a half at least. The asphalt was hot, and getting hotter as the sun continued to beat down. His feet were getting hot too. Walking at this pace on bare feet was not going to be an option, so he accelerated into a quick jog, trying to keep on his toes to minimise the impact and reduce the burning.

He was grateful to reach the shade of the building but once he'd done so he had to stop for a few minutes to catch his breath and let his burning feet cool down.

Oddly, there was very little sign of life. Eric walked as far around the brick building as he could. It was huge, much bigger than the football stadium in Liverpool he'd circumnavigated what seemed like years ago. Eventually, and on the far side of the building to where he'd entered, was a large glass sliding door. He walked up to it to peer inside. Eric was starting to feel really confident. He'd managed to sneak up to one of the most protected buildings on the planet and no-one had raised so much as an eyebrow. And that's when the automatic sensor picked him up, opening the main entrance glass doors as wide as they could possibly go and he was confronted by over a dozen well-armed, highly-trained and very secretive soldiers who all immediately turned to look directly at him, weapons drawn.

Instinctively, Eric froze. Then, one by one, the soldiers started to holster their weapons. One or two edged towards him, seemingly staring him right in the eye. Eric backed away from the door. They inched closer, looking puzzled, but as they reached the door one of the men started to fiddle with the sensor that had picked him up. Eric snuck as deftly as he could between the soldiers and was inside.

Eric may have watched too many films, but he had assumed a building like this would have increasingly impenetrable layers of security, leading to a central point where all the really secret stuff was stored, but it didn't. What he found was a boring, open plan office with clerks, and secretaries and people goofing off by printers and water coolers, just like in his old call centre back home. In the main lobby was a large reception desk with staff tapping away at computers, answering phones and generally being busy. At the far end of the office was a large set of double doors, and people were coming in and out of those, and assuming he wouldn't find any hidden aliens in Lisa from Accounts' packed lunch, he headed towards them.

Once there, it was only ten seconds or so before someone pushed the left hand door open and stepped inside what appeared to be a well-lit corridor. A middle-aged, well-dressed man held the door open, at first Eric thought he was holding it for him, but then he noticed someone else walking towards it, a good twenty paces away. He grabbed the opportunity and ghosted past him into the fluorescent-lit corridor.

The corridor was wide. Perhaps twenty yards left to right and disappeared to a point way off in the distance like converging train tracks. Eric had never been inside a building so large. He checked the clock on the wall – 10:15am, so he'd been moving for a little over two hours at this point. He had banked on Jane agreeing to pick him up once she had calmed down and he didn't want to keep Jane waiting by losing track of time. He assumed parking outside this facility for any length of time would draw unnecessary attention, so he vowed to get in, have a good look around, and be outside well before sunset.

Eric set off down the corridor, as usual keeping tight to the side to avoid the handful of people walking up and down. Occasionally electric golf buggies would silently whirr past him in either direction. He was tempted to hop onto the back of one but didn't think he could manage it without alerting the driver. Most carried boxes, but occasionally a uniformed military officer was on board, all medals and firm jawline. Eric was trying to figure out how on earth this corridor could be so long compared to the length of the building he had seen from outside when it dawned on him that he was heading – very gradually – down a slope, and therefore must be going underground.

After a good thirty minute walk, he started to see the end of the corridor. The end of the train tracks. Ahead of him was a door, around ten yards wide, and it was open.

Eric got to the door and peered around the corner. Through the door was what he would later best describe as an enormous indoor aircraft hangar. It was big enough to hold three jumbo jets and as high as it was wide. Fluorescent day lighting hung from the ceiling and the room felt warm, but not hot. There must have been fifty people, mostly wearing civilian clothes (the ubiquitous chinos and polo shirts) and a handful in army uniform. Not fatigues, but proper officer class stuff. Most had ipads and some were earnestly looking at gauges and dials and tapping the glass of the thirty five or so tanks that were scattered around the hangar. Right in the middle of the building was what could be described as the money shot. A silver disc, at least thirty yards in diameter, surrounded by what appeared to be iron bars. It was rotating and humming slowly, about ten feet off the floor.

Oddly, no-one was paying this much attention. Eric walked over to it, transfixed. There was a red LED display on a plinth underneath it. This read "77:07:09:14:10". The "10" then flicked over to an "11". Eric counted the seconds in his head, his eyes fixed on the display. As he reached fifty-eight, it flicked to "12". 77 years ago was 1947, give or take. Roswell. 'Oh my giddy aunt', thought Eric. The rumours were true and the whack job conspiracy theorists were right. It immediately made him wonder what else was being hidden from the public, and in that moment he planned to find out.

A spinning disc meant nothing, of course. Well – it meant something, but for all he knew this could be somewhere they bring VIPs to convince them to keep investing in this place. A cool art installation that generated billions in government funding. It dawned on Eric that he was turning into something of a cynic, and he was learning to trust no-one. He looked around, and headed to one of the glass tanks that wasn't being inspected by a badly-dressed golfer. Empty.

Eric checked another, and another. Most were empty. Some had rock samples in, but he couldn't see any sign of E.T or his mates. By now, he'd seen inside most of the tanks. The largest was right at the back of the room, and surrounded by soldiers and he started walking towards it for a closer look.

That's when Eric saw it, and this time something was absolutely, unquestionably staring. Not at the soldiers, not at the spinning saucer, not even at the huge chunk of meat that had just been lowered into its cage. Whatever this thing was, it was staring right at Eric Curtis.

Thirty

The big tank was about the size of the RV he'd jumped out of a few hours ago. It was on a raised plinth, so the staff's chests were level with the bottom of the glass. This one had both thick glass and steel bars and large, angry scratches all down the inside of both. Eric was no more than ten yards away from it. He noticed a quiet buzz of excitement and the crowd starting to gravitate towards the glass, eyes all looking up, expectedly. He'd never seen anything like this.

He'd assumed any alien would look like the old trope of a skinny body with a huge head and bulging eyes, but that was more like one of the giant lumps of grease he'd pulled out of the drain back home. It had what Eric guessed that passed as its nose pressed to the glass, and it was the ugliest creature he'd seen since Toto. A single angry eye piercing into his, a razor-toothed malevolent smile gurning from what he assumed was its mouth, a slimy, bony finger pointing straight at him, and an ear-piercing guttural wail that filled the enormous hangar emanating from deep inside its belly.

Oh bloody hell. This started to feel like a huge mistake. Eric hadn't even considered the remote possibility that if there was life on Mars locked up down here that they'd sense or see him. And this one without question could. "GET OUT!", Eric screamed to himself. "GET OUT NOW"

The hairs on the back of Eric's neck were standing up. His knees buckled and he felt like he was going to throw up. He was utterly terrified. Frozen in fear, he could sense his brain shutting down and his bladder starting to contract. "GETOUTGETOUTGETOUT" reverberated through his brain like a bell. Eric's mind suddenly snapped into action.

People began following the trajectory of the pointing finger to where Eric was standing and he didn't think it would be long before someone started wondering what was making it so excited and move towards him. Whatever this thing was, it wasn't from earth. It gave the impression of being able to break out of its cage at will so Eric decided perhaps now was the time to listen to the voice and get out.

The staff were now chattering excitedly, and everyone seemed to be either punching stuff into their iPads or making frantic phone calls. A giant orange light started flashing by the door and a loud buzzing alarm sounded. That felt like Eric's cue to get the hell out of Dodge. He turned and sprinted for the hangar door as it started to close, taking one last look at the mayhem behind him. The thing was now bouncing up and down, screaming in furious anger and pointing at Eric as he slipped, unnoticed by the humans in the room into the corridor.

He legged it. There were lots of people from the office running towards the hangar, clearly interested in the commotion. Eric imagined this thing hadn't behaved like this before he heard snippets of conversations as he ran back up the corridor:

"So it wasn't hibernating. This is gonna freak the General out"

"Lock the facility down. No-one in, and no-one out"

"Have they turned on the language translator yet?".

The what now? This couldn't be good. If they actually had one of those and could speak to it,

Eric's cover was about to be blown. He quickened from a run to an all-out sprint, running back up the gradual incline, dodging people who were hurrying towards the hanger to see what the fuss was about. Eric ran all the way to the doors he'd had held open for him before. Just before he reached them he sourly noticed a door on the left with the words "JFK evidence room" stencilled onto the glass. He just had time to mutter a quiet "oh for fuck's sake" before popping back into the open plan office and straight out through the front doors that slid mercifully and effortlessly open for him.

The front doors were now wide open but the pandemonium going on behind Eric still prevented anyone from giving a shit. The order for total lockdown hadn't reached this area yet but he didn't think it would be long until it did. He was still running when he got to the main gate which he ducked under without breaking stride. The guards in the sentry box were yakking away on the phone, probably cursing their luck they were on guard duty outside and not watching the utter mayhem that was going on in the main building. The buzzing alarms and klaxons had stopped but Eric watched as soldiers raced about through the main doors, weapons drawn and barking into walkie talkies.

It couldn't have been long past noon and the sun was roasting the road into a hot, shimmering, tacky lava. This was going to be a long wait and Eric wasn't sure his feet (or arse) would stand being welded into the tarmac for long.

He decided to hunker down behind the guard hut in a tiny patch of shadow and wait. It would be at least six hours unless he could think of a plan B. Walking back to Las Vegas was definitely not an option. He'd be dead from heatstroke in a matter of minutes.

Eric couldn't think of a plan B.

The wait was excruciating. Eric decided to try and play some mental games to stimulate him. He was going to guess the colour of the next car to drive past.

Ten minutes or so later, not a single car had driven past and he began contemplating just walking back to Las Vegas after all.

Then, in the distance, the unmistakable sight of a car, the sun glinting off its windscreen and dust being kicked up in its wake. Blue. The car would be blue. How exciting. Eric tried to imagine how comfortable the driver would be, sitting in his air conditioned car, sipping from an ice cold bottle of water, humming along to music on the radio. He wished he could be whoever was driving the car for the next day or so, just to get away from this hot earth and painful cramps.

The car wasn't blue. It was silver. And it stopped right outside the guard hut. About three feet from where Eric was sitting. Dust kicking up off the shoulder of the road and engine still running. The door opened and he could hear the wonderful sound of the air-conditioning on full blast, but unfortunately for Eric, the exhaust was pointing at his face, blowing boiling fumes straight at him. It made the sticky air even more unpleasant if that were possible.

A smartly dressed man got out and popped the boot. He went round and retrieved a briefcase, leaving it open. This suddenly seemed very odd indeed. Eric wondered if he should make a break for it, when he started to speak to the guards in a very posh English accent:

"Excuse me chaps", he started. "Have you seen this man anywhere?" and he brandished a photo towards them. Eric could make out the face of a very well-known and notorious British TV celebrity who had recently been exposed as a paedophile. What on earth....?

"His name is Eric, and he's what we in England would call an absolute fucking knob-headed twat with the intellect of frog spawn and he was last seen on this road having escaped from a mental asylum. We want to find him before he does anything stupid, like try and break in here". The guards stiffened, not really understanding this weird Englishman and told him no, no-one would be that dumb and they haven't seen anyone all day. At least, Eric assumed that's what they said because by then he was hiding in the boot ready for an almighty bollocking off Andy and Rachel which he was pretty sure was on its way.

The driver thanked the men, threw the briefcase aggressively into the boot, where it connected squarely with Eric's ribcage, and slammed the boot shut before driving away, making sure he hit every bump and pothole he could find. He turned the radio up to full volume, and noisily sang along to the unmistakeable lyrics of 'Fuck You' by Ce-Lo Green. After a few minutes, a mobile phone rang and in the darkness Eric managed to open the briefcase and press the green button to answer the call.

As expected, it was Andy. And he was not a happy bunny.

"Curtis you total arse" was the greeting as Eric answered. "I cannot emphasise the stupidity of what you've done". He was yelling. Eric could sense the rage and the phone grew hot against his ear.

"Of course we were monitoring the RV. I should have guessed you'd go off and do something stupid". Andy was apoplectic. "You have jeopardised everything, you could have blown your cover and then we're all fucked. You have put Jane in extreme danger and nearly damaged the intelligence gathering relationship we've had with our closest and most powerful ally". Those are the bits Eric caught, as the invective was flowing. There were a few 'twats, cunts, idiots, pricks and fucktards' thrown in too, and Eric couldn't be specific about all the words as he was still being bounced around in the boot of this blue car. Or was it silver?

Eric was wordlessly dropped off by Andy's man in Nevada at the private section of the airport where Jane was tearfully waiting for him. They'd got to her within an hour of dropping Eric off that morning and diverted her straight there. The jet was fuelled and the plane was off minutes later, back to London. Eric found his grey tracksuit and beanie and slipped them on.

Jane looked at Eric angrily. "Well? Was it worth it?" she asked

Eric grinned. He hated getting yelled at but nodded and whispered in her ear "I'll tell you when we're somewhere that isn't bugged".

The plane landed in London and Eric was dragged to Andy's office and given a two hour spittle-laden lecture on what a hopeless little specimen he was. It was horrific. Now Eric could understand why soldiers caved in under interrogation. Hand him an orange jumpsuit and ten minutes with Andy and he would tell you everything he knew.

"Andy, I'm really sorry. I promise it will never happen again. Never".

"Bloody right it won't Curtis. You're not going home again until we're finished with you. And so we're completely clear, this could be a million years from now. Got it?" Andy's face was red with rage.

Eric slunk back to his quarters. Unsurprisingly, Jane was nowhere to be seen and his phone had been removed. The beer was gone from the fridge and the doors now only opened from the outside.

Thirty One

And so began formal training. Eric was effectively under house arrest. Rachel was nowhere to be seen, Andy never came to visit and Colin never breezily appeared swinging his car keys asking if he wanted to go home.

Eric was given a strict schedule to follow. Exercise in the morning with some running and weights and basic tradecraft skills training in the afternoons. Meals were simple, plain and healthy. No more fried delights, no alcohol and no caffeine. He embraced this with vigour. Eric enjoyed the exercise, running hard and eating well. He assumed he was being watched and his performance was being measured and he wanted to impress Andy to get back into his good books.

The afternoon training included a combination of basic weapon training and hand to hand combat skills and more theoretical studies like map reading and basic languages. Eric never asked, and was never told how long this would last. He had decided very early to knuckle down and just get on with it, hoping he'd eventually be allowed out for good behaviour.

Eric started to wonder what this training was for. A specific mission, or just to make him a more effective operative for a multitude of tasks that were coming? He decided not to ask as he wasn't sure he'd like the answer.

Days became weeks, and weeks became a month. Eric missed Jane, Oscar and Kate dreadfully. He missed Toto. He missed his old life and sometimes dreamed of driving on the M4 listening to the radio and the simple banality of what he'd left behind. He reflected that you never really know what you have until it's gone.

After a month had passed, he had a visit from Andy Barnes. Eric had returned from the gym to have his lunch and found Andy sitting in his quarters, waiting for him.

"Eric. Good to see you 'looking' so well" he began. It was the first time Eric had been called by his first name since returning from Area 51. "Just checking in on you. You're making good progress. Your trainers say your work rate and attitude is spot on. Keep it up. Oh, and Jane says hello"

Eric bristled at this. "Where is she? Where are the kids" he asked. He made sure not to sound aggressive or angry. He knew he wasn't in a place to put any demands on Andy.

"They're at home, he replied. They miss you and asked me to say hello for them. You'll be able to see them in a few days. But I wanted to come and have a chat with you just to make sure you've learned your lesson and you really do understand what we expect from you, ok?"

"Yes", said Eric. "I understand. I really am sorry for being a tit. I promise it will never happen again".

"Good" replied Andy. "This is serious stuff we're doing Eric. It changes the world, and for the better. It makes it a safer place. It's not a game. You are truly unique and if we lose you to some daft caper then we'll lose an opportunity we'll almost certainly not have again in our lifetime. Now, there will be another few weeks of training and we'll have some news for you, ok"

"No problem Andy, whatever you say".

Andy tapped on the door which swung open. As he walked through the door he turned and said "You're still on the shit list. Remember that. There are things coming up that could help you get off it. Do as you're told, don't be a dickhead and we'll work out a plan to get you home"

The word 'home' hung in the air. Eric felt another pang of sadness for his family. He wondered what they'd be doing at that moment and vowed that when all this was over he'd never take his life for granted again.

Thirty Two

Two more weeks went by. Eric had been eating right and training hard for six weeks. He could feel his stomach was starting to get toned for the first time in thirty years and could comfortably run fifteen miles without a break. He could not only shoot a pistol but could dismantle and rebuild it in under a minute. Not blindfolded, but he didn't think that would ever be necessary. He had become proficient enough in self defence and had learned a handful of useful phrases in French, Spanish and Arabic.

Eric was in his room on a Tuesday morning, finishing his steamed chicken and rice lunch, when Andy and Rachel walked in. He looked up nervously as he pushed a fork of food into his mouth. "Morning Andy, Rachel" he managed to say between chews. They look stern faced. "You're not here to tell me I'm going home, are you" he asked, sadly.

"No Eric, we're not", replied Rachel. She sat next to him and opened a leather file. It was very thick and Eric recognised the picture on the first page immediately. The remnants of the chicken suddenly stuck in his throat, and he reached for a glass of water.

Rachel waited until Eric had stopped choking and began to speak.

"The American presidential election is on the horizon Eric. We've had over three years of the current one, and it's fair to say the world is in a bit of a mess because of him and heading for real danger. What we're about to tell you is so beyond top secret it's difficult to put it into words. I'm afraid this mission is utterly non-negotiable. You are our only option and compliance is mandatory. It's going to be very dangerous, and there is a chance you won't make it out alive. Now, we'll do all we can to protect you but you're going to be totally alone with a lot of this. Before we proceed, do you understand?

"I understand" said Eric. "I don't think I'm going to like this very much, am I?"

"No" interjected Andy. "You're not going to like it one bit".

Eric slumped in his chair. He tried to think of something clever to say but his mouth was dry and his throat was tightening. And he didn't feel particularly clever right now.

"What we're asking you to do is important" went on Andy. "It's going to change the course of history. It's vital for the safety and security of the UK, and if we succeed, we'll be saving millions of lives and preventing a war".

Eric sat silently, trying to take this in.

"Now, the president will win the next election. Easily". Said Rachel. She personified calmness and confidence. "The problem is, we know he's compromised. Badly. The Russians and the Chinese have managed to obtain some very personal information about him. And it's all true. We know it's true, and don't ask how. It doesn't matter what that information is, suffice to say the president does not want these details to be made public. It would do more than discredit him. It would make the USA a laughing stock and it leaves him open to blackmail. He is too arrogant to simply not stand for election and believes that he can pay his way out of it by buying back the evidence and hoping his enemies will simply never make it public"

"So what do they want to get out of this?" asked Eric

"They want trade deals. New oil drilling rights. A reduction in American military interventions in countries they have an interest in. Access to American markets for technology so they can plant trackers in American computers. They want to reduce America's global influence and expand communism to existing democracies in Asia and Eastern Europe" said Andy, sternly.

"Would that be so bad?" asked Eric. "Surely congress wouldn't let those things happen?"

Rachel stepped in. "He's going to win by a landslide. His opponents are still fighting between themselves and the Americans love a strong leader. He'll have absolute power in government and by the time the public see what's happening it will be too late. These are not reversable policies".

Andy continued "Not only will we see the price of gas and oil rocket, but we'd be defenceless against any invasion in Eastern Europe without American help. There would be a cold war again, and potentially an actual ground war which would start in the Baltic and spread west. People will die. Lots of people".

This sounded totally plausible. Eric could feel a sense of dread spreading through him.

"And I'm guessing you don't want me to sneak into the Kremlin and steal this evidence and destroy it? Because that would be easier than what I think you're suggesting" pleaded Eric.

"No", Andy and Rachel replied in unison.

"So you want me to do something to the president that would make him change his mind about standing?" Asked Eric hopefully.

"No", came the reply again.

Eric laughed "Ah, then you want me to *kill* the president?". He slapped his thigh for comedic effect, hoping they'd laugh along with him at the sheer absurdity of the suggestion.

"Yes". Said Andy. "That is exactly what we want you to do".

No-one said anything for what seemed an age. Eric sat, unblinking, trying to take it all in.

It was a good few minutes before Eric started to speak. Andy hadn't moved a muscle and was waiting for his reaction. His poker face gave nothing away.

"No". Said Eric. "Absolutely not".

"Yes". Replied Andy. "Absolutely yes. You seem to think you have choices. You don't. This is the way it has to be. It's already been decided. We can't possibly allow any of this to happen. And if he is elected, it will. We know this to be true".

Rachel spoke next. "Eric, the people you've killed so far. They were bastards. You were brilliant. You did each job because you knew it had to be done. This has to be done. He's a sociopath. Millions could die. Just because he doesn't want the world to know what he does in his spare time. And believe me, if you knew what that was you'd want to kill him anyway".

Eric protested "But this is the most heavily protected man in the world. I wouldn't get within fifty yards of him before I got shot. Even if I wanted to kill him, which I don't, it won't be possible".

"Eric, he's a bastard. You have to trust me on this. I've seen things. I know things. Kill him for us. You'll be doing more good than you could possibly imagine. I promise you that". Said Andy.

Eric sat, trying to take it all in. He starting thinking about how he could turn this to his advantage when Andy spoke again. "This will be the last thing we ask of you. You'll be out after this. I'll give that to you in writing. We'll pay you, of course. Whatever you want"

"I'm listening" said Eric, his curiosity piqued.

"Ok, you won't pay tax again. Ever. We'll put you on a nice pension. Sort you and Jane out with a house. Maybe upgrade that bike of yours" replied Andy. "And we'll fund Jane's shelter so it never needs to worry about cash again. Ever".

"Keep talking", said Eric

"Say yes". Said Andy. "And we'll talk"

Eric knew it didn't matter what he asked for. He was going to do it. A combination of the cash coupled with the convincing argument about world peace meant Eric was always going to do it. He'd probably have done it for nothing if it meant getting home to his family. Andy should have opened with that offer, he thought.

"Yes. Fuck it". Said Eric, "you gotta die of something, right?". He hoped this would lighten the mood. It didn't.

"See you at 8am tomorrow for the briefing", said Rachel. "and thanks".

As they got up to leave, Eric stood up. "I need this in writing Andy. I'm sorry but that's how it has to be. The money, the tax, the house, everything. And the get out clause. Otherwise I'm not doing it".

"Sure thing" said Andy. "Sure thing".

Thirty Three

"Ok, let me get this straight. You want me to break into the White House, sneak into the President's bedroom, slit his throat while he sleeps and escape before the Secret Service even know I've been there?" Eric asked, once the initial briefing was over.

Eric's signed letter confirming the deal was folded and tucked in his back pocket.

"Yes. That's about the size of it" replied Andy, without a smile. "There will be lots of training, and you'll have lots of help from some very switched on people. We've modelled the different likely scenarios and we firmly believe that the risk is minimal. It needs to look like his wife has done it - domestic murder will be easier to explain away than an assassin striking at the heart of the greatest democracy on the globe, and the most protected man alive".

Eric asked "Andy, who has sanctioned this? Who knows?

Andy's reply was both alarming and cryptic in equal measure. "Eric, all I can say is that there are forces at work who are making decisions so far above even my paygrade that to even question them would mean I'd be working in the Falklands sweeping up penguin shit by the weekend. However, I was told that if we'd been able to kill Hitler before 1940 it would have saved millions of lives, and this mission is something similar. I'd ask if you were still in, but

I'm afraid I'm not even giving you the illusion of a choice. You're in".

Andy confirmed Colin would pick Eric up the following morning and drive him to the airport. "I'll be at the plane and will meet you there for further briefing and to go over your training plan as we fly out to the RV point"

Colin was waiting at 9am on the dot – in yet another shiny new car. He drove them in silence to the airport. It felt like everything had been dialled up a notch. Colin was on edge. Eric wondered how much he knew, but didn't want to ask. Plausible deniability. Colin's grim face and tight grip on the steering wheel gave the air in the car a claustrophobic, breathless feel and Eric could feel his stomach tightening as approached the airport. For once, he was praying the roadworks would be in full effect and they'd be delayed for long enough that someone senior would sober up and decide that this was a really, really bad idea. Obviously this was the day when the M4 contraflow was miraculously removed and they coasted all the way to the airport at 70mph.

They cruised into the airport by a small service road, a military guard snapping to attention as the car approached, not even pausing to check the occupant's identities but opening the gates and allowing them to speed through. They drove onto the runway and straight to the steps of a waiting jet.

Rachel was waiting by the plane with Andy. Eric was relieved to see Will there too - his stargazing mate from the Middle East. They were all dressed in chinos and open shirts - like a management team on an away day. Eric was in his usual jogging pants and sweatshirt, beanie and sunglasses. They boarded the jet, buckled up and took off. As usual, Rachel was straight down to business. They went over the plan. Although it was quite simple, they must have walked through it a dozen times, until Eric could recite it without notes and had visualised every detail in his head. He was reassured by Will's confidence but it felt fraught with extreme dangers at every turn. There would be a plethora of cameras, dogs, alarms and about 60 highly trained secret service armed guards who would all be trying to stop Eric getting in, and more importantly, getting out, and not afraid to use deadly force without even stopping to think.

The plane touched down at Dulles airport at 5am. It was dark and cold. Eric's teammates went through the diplomatic channel in the terminal building while he walked through the cargo area where it had been accurately predicted there were no infrared cameras and all the dogs were on leads. The airport was still eerily quiet and Eric slipped through unnoticed.

The team agreed to meet on the 267 expressway which meant Eric would need to clamber through a few fields and marshes and over a couple of highway barriers. The ubiquitous BMW purred to a gentle stop on the hard shoulder twenty minutes later. Will popped the boot and Eric climbed in, before clambering through a gap in the seat to join the others.

"For fuck's sake" complained Eric. "I'm cold and wet, I've been walking through God knows what and Christ knows how many worms and slugs I've trodden on. Still, at least you lot are dry and warm"

"Oh fucking pack it in Eric" said Will. "You walked across a field in the rain, it's hardly a minefield under enemy fire now, is it?".

Eric, feeling like a twat, packed it in.

"Now put some clothes on. That's Nappa leather your wet arse is dripping on". Will was not a man who seemed in the mood to take Eric's complaints seriously. "We're an hour out. Buckle up, sit down, and shut up".

This caused Rachel to laugh. "This is our prized asset Will" She said. Treat him with the respect he deserves".

"Oh, I am" said Will. "I absolutely am".

The BMW drove through Washington to the British Embassy and as at the airport in London the barriers parted as it approached. Will eased through the gates, parking underground. The staff had just started to arrive but they seemed to go unnoticed. The ambassador had been recalled to London for an urgent meeting for a few days so the team used his private rooms as their base and began unpacking the kit. The building was amazing. High ceilings, stunning art on every wall, thick carpets and heavy doors that glided effortlessly open with the gentlest of pushes. Andy wrote a note for Eric. It read 'The whole building is bugged - don't even speak. No-one can know you're even here'.

Eric grabbed his pen and replied underneath 'Russians or Chinese?'. He scribbled some more. "The Americans. They bug all the embassies". He whispered in Eric's ear "of course, they know we know. And we know they know we know - it's all a bit of a game. Just go with it". Right. Not only could Eric not be seen, now he couldn't be heard either.

He scribbled the word 'cameras?' and Andy shook his head.

The plan was for Eric to have a practice run that night. Even if the opportunity arose, he was, under no circumstances, to engage the President. Everyone would meet afterwards for a full debrief to confirm the plan was solid, and that they had the go-ahead from the people making the decision. Eric tried to figure out who was behind this but decided he didn't need or want to know.

Thirty Four

At 1am, Will popped out in the most boring, nondescript car Eric had ever seen, with the cover story if anyone asked, to get a burrito. They reached a diner a mile or so from the White House and he pulled up alongside the kerb. As he opened his door, Eric climbed over him, making sure he dragged his arse across Will's face, knowing he couldn't flinch or make a sound. Eric was sure he'd pay for that later and he knew Will would be wondering what kind of child they were sending in to do something so difficult and dangerous.

Washington - like most American cities - is essentially a load of straight roads, so finding 1600 Pennsylvania Avenue was very easy. At 1:50am it was still lit up like a Newcastle night club and Eric stood outside for a few minutes just to gather his thoughts and get his bearings. The building was smaller than he had imagined and the huge American flag fluttered gently in the early autumn breeze. It was a typically cold night but Eric didn't feel it. His palms were sweaty and he welcomed the cool air which provided some relief to his nervous energy. He made his way down to the west of the building, found a point where the railings were joined to a wall, and hopped over. Although there was no alarm, Eric knew the sensors would be going crazy, so, as planned, he sprinted over to the outdoor pool and dropped into the shallow end, standing in ankle deep water. Now he was cold. He had to tense every muscle to stop himself shaking and creating ripples in the water.

Fifteen seconds later, lights came on and dogs came out, followed by both secret service and soldiers in uniform, guns drawn. The dogs were going crazy but couldn't pick up a scent past the chlorinated water in the swimming pool. Some barked at the water's edge of the unlit pool but a sweep of the area with torches confirmed nothing was there. Satisfied it was a false alarm, everyone began to holster their weapons and started to make their way back inside.

The dogs were put back into the guard house with their handlers, so that appeared to be one less thing to worry about tonight.

As the retinue of secret service staff started to move out of earshot, Eric was up and out of the pool and running hard behind them, catching up just as the last of the soldiers went into the White House. It was cold with the water running down his skin but the adrenalin was pumping faster than ever so he felt ok. His feet had dried in the grass, so he was happy he wouldn't be leaving footprints. Eric closely followed the last guard through the open door which clicked shut behind him.

Eric stood against the wall in the lobby beyond the door and listened to the soldiers debriefing their boss about the incident he'd caused. Another false alarm was the consensus. The fact that they'd reacted so quickly and assertively removed all feelings of complacency though. He knew this wasn't going to be 'a piece of piss'. It was going to be huge vat of the stuff.

After the hubbub and excitement had died down, Eric decided to move.

He kept tight to the wall as he went. Through the archway and into the press room. The team had assumed this would be empty and it was the route with the fewest doors - which should be the easiest way to go unnoticed. Eric crept past the cabinet room and up the two flights of stairs and into the centre hall of the private living quarters. He checked the time on the clock in the corridor. 2:15am. There were sweeps from the security detail every twenty minutes so he stood next to the clock and waited for the next one to pass. He slowed his breathing and checked his pulse. He initially panicked when he calculated it to be 120bpm, but then realised he need to multiply it by six, not ten, so it was normal. High, but no panic. Eric tried to calm himself down as he could tell he wasn't thinking straight. He took some deep breaths, thought of Kate and Oscar and let his mind settle. He imagined them bickering about which TV channel to watch. He thought of the pair of them getting ready for bed and hoped they'd brush their teeth and switch their phones off. He realised he'd never thought such things before, and it calmed him.

The guard passed. Lazily sweeping a torch from left to right he walked right past Eric, moving within two feet of where he was standing. He stretched, yawned, farted, and chuckled to himself as he did so.

As he disappeared round a corner and out of view, Eric moved west, past the yellow oval room and into the Presidential living room. He opened the door just enough to slip inside and let it click softly behind him. Eric stood in the darkness, waiting for his eyes to adjust to the gloom. As soon as he was confident he could move across the room without banging into a table, he did so, and pressed himself up against the far wall when the door swung open and the farting guard lazily threw a beam of light around the living room. He didn't check behind any furniture or the door - in contrast to his mates downstairs who were thorough and switched on. Eric hoped he was on duty tomorrow night when he was doing this for real.

Eric waited a few minutes for the guard to have fully moved away before climbing the small flight of stairs that led to the main bedroom. The door was slightly ajar, so he pushed it open and snuck inside.

The room was gently lit with the lamps from the garden throwing just enough light through the windows for Eric to see what was going on. The curtains were wide open and the familiar face of the President of the United States was lying facing him as he entered the room. What wasn't so familiar was the figure lying next to him. Clearly not his wife, Eric was puzzled. Where was the First Lady and who was this? This person had short hair, was very slightly built and no more than five feet tall. Eric peered closer and could just about make out that she wad East Asian, possibly a Chinese girl. Probably no older than eighteen. She was lying, eyes open, but very obviously not awake. At first, he thought she was dead, but Eric could just about make out shallow breaths on her semi-covered chest. He took in all of this detail, knowing he'd be quizzed later. Eric had a quick look around the rooms, making sure the letter opener Andy had promised would be there, actually was. After a quick search, he found it sitting on his desk in the living room.

As Eric stood at the desk, turning the letter opener over in his hand, he heard a noise behind him. He spun round to see the President of the United States, naked, mouth wide open and eyes transfixed in a dazed stare, trying to figure out how his letter opener was moving, mid-air, unaided. He froze. Oh shit.

He rubbed his eyes, which was Eric's opportunity to place it gently back on the desk and get out of there. He quickly walked over to the living room door that led back to the corridor while the president walked over to the desk and held the letter opener up to the window. He flicked on the desk lamp and looked around. Seeing nothing, and with a confused expression on his face, he pressed a button and twenty seconds later his living room door flew open with two guards, guns drawn, bolted inside.

"Sorry boys, got a bit spooked" said the President. "I thought I saw something but think I was sleepwalking there".

"It's ok Sir, step aside, let us check the room" said guard number one. All business, there was no messing about and farting with this guy.

The President glanced nervously towards his bedroom. "Ok boys, no need to check the bedroom, I'll go back to bed. Stand down".

"Sir", commanded guard number one, "please step aside and let us check the room. You know we have protocols to observe"

The President walked back into his bedroom and slammed his door shut. Eric could just make out a muffled "Observe my ass, you pair of pricks". He snuck through the open door and back into the corridor. The guards followed behind him.

"Jesus, he is such a massive tool. Why do we risk our lives for this guy?" Said the first.

"The job Jim, it's the job", replied the second. "It's better than protecting some foreign ambassador in the Middle East, right?"

"I don't know about that" the first guard. "At least over there you know who the enemy is. Anyway, where is the First Lady tonight?"

"He sent her away to Florida so he could *work*, remember". The intonation sounded obvious to Eric. "Why? Who's he got in there tonight? Asked the guard

"Someone imported again, probably" replied number one. "I don't know why his wife puts up with it". Somewhere in the recess of Eric's brain, a penny dropped about the contents of a Russian dossier.

Getting out was relatively easy when compared to getting in. Eric simply followed the guards back down to the main lobby, and waited by the door for someone to walk through. As a guard went out for a smoke he slipped past him into the night air, ran down the main path outside the building and ducked under the barrier. The alarm sounded but by the time the guards had scrambled again Eric was on the main road. The rendezvous point was the

Beacon Hotel. Dead north of the White House and impossible to miss. Eric was standing by the staff entrance at 3:30am, when bang on time a car pulled up and the driver stepped out to check his tyres, leaving the door open. Eric threw himself in and collapsed in the passenger seat. The friendly face of Will swept in beside him. He gave Eric a smile and said "hello beautiful" and then punched him in the arm. "And that's payback for the arse in the face trick earlier".

Will took a very long route back to the embassy, swapping cars twice and making sure they weren't followed. As Will told Eric on the way back, they had to minimise all risks, otherwise there would be war. He hadn't considered this until now. If the Americans had suspected the Brits had murdered their President, or were even planning to, despite him being a mindless, bigoted old fool, there would probably be consequences.

They pulled into the basement of the Thompson Washington, a nondescript hotel in the South East of the city at 4:30am. Andy and Rachel were there to greet them and wanted an immediate debrief.

"We're not going back to the embassy?" asked Eric.

"Don't be stupid" replied Andy, "it's bugged, remember? Christ, can't you take anything on board?" For the first time since they'd met, Andy seemed tense and on edge. He mumbled a "sorry, that was unkind".

Eric followed them to a suite where Will also joined the party. They sat down, Rachel handing Eric some clothes. He pulled them on and sat down.

"Ok, line by line. What happened", asked Andy

Eric finished his summary of the evening's events. There was silence in the room. Rachel, who had been making notes, put her pen down and looked at Andy.

"Shit". She said

"I know, I know" replied Andy

"What? What did I miss?" asked Eric. He guessed he'd done something catastrophically wrong.

"Shit". Repeated Andy.

Rachel scribbled some more notes. More silence.

"Hey, if I screwed up, tell me. I'm doing my best here" pleaded Eric

Andy spoke first. "We should have done it tonight" He began. "Having what sounds like a prostitute to blame is almost too perfect. God knows when he'll have another one in there". Rachel nodded in agreement.

"Shit", said Eric. "I'm sorry. I'm so sorry, I didn't..". Andy interrupted Eric with a wave of his hand

"Jesus Eric, you've spent years working in call centres. Making an executive decision on the timing and manner of the assassination of the leader of the free world isn't something we'd expect you to do. We should have planned for this eventuality, and we didn't. We'll make sure you have better intelligence next time."

Eric coughed. "Next time?"

"The mission is to eliminate the president. It's done, when it's done. Now, anything else before we call it a night?". Andy gave the impression he didn't want any more questions.

"Well, one" replied Eric, resigned to his role. "The girl. In the room. She didn't look much older than Kate. Can you find out if she's alright?"

"I'll make some discreet enquiries" said Andy. "but not at the expense of this operation".

Thirty Five

Eric woke just after 8am. He went to his door and, checking no-one was around, pulled his breakfast tray inside and tucked into his crispy bacon and powdered egg. It tasted better than the steamed chicken and rice he'd been eating in London.

After breakfast he showered, flicked on the TV and settled in for a boring afternoon. Eric had learned his lesson. Answer when called. That was it. Room service lunch followed and more TV. Sitting on the bed, he flicked through the channels, his eyes got heavy and soon he was fast asleep. He was in the middle of a dream when he was violently shaken awake.

"What time is it?" asked Eric, wearily.

"Time to get up and go. Now" replied Will.

Eric's eyes snapped awake. It was dusk outside. His small bag had been packed and a set of clothes was folded neatly on the chair. "Now". Will repeated.

Eric dressed quickly and followed Will down the corridor and through a service entrance and he jumped into the front passenger seat of the car that had bought him to the hotel the previous night. As they accelerated through the car park Eric heard a gentle cough from behind.

He turned to see Andy and Rachel sitting in the back seat, papers and folders on their laps, and worried looks on their faces.

Eric was now fully awake. "Where are we going?" he asked

"Andrew's Air Force base" replied Will. "We'll be there in 20"

Eric thought of home. "Is there a plane waiting for me?" he asked, hopefully.

"Errr, yes, in a manner of speaking", replied Rachel. "It's Air Force One".

"We have an issue with timing", continued Andy. The president has suddenly decided he's going to Russia. This evening. He's set up a private meeting with the Russian president, and we believe he's going to do a secret deal on this dossier business. That simply cannot be allowed to happen"

"I'm going to Russia?" asked Eric

"No. And neither is the president, if all goes to plan" replied Andy

"And what is the plan"? Asked Eric. Desperation now obvious in his voice. He was pretty sure he wasn't going to like this answer.

"We're working on it" interjected Rachel. "Give us a minute"

For the first time since he'd been working with MI6, Eric lost his temper. "Working on it?" He spluttered. "You're WORKING ON IT?". He was shouting now. "We get to the plane in 20 minutes and you don't have a fucking plan? What am I going to do? Kill the pilot or blow up the plane? Either way I'm guessing I'm about to become expendable?"

"Shush Eric, I'm working on it". Rachel's brow furrowed as she made even more notes on the papers she was reading.

Eric looked at Rachel's folder. She had an outline of a big aeroplane and was scribbling furiously in the margins of the page.

"Will, pull over here. This will do." Will did as Rachel had asked and eased the car into a Burger King. "Right Eric, listen carefully. Time is not our friend today". Eric listened carefully. Very carefully.

Thirty Six

Eric got out of the car in the Burger King car park with Andy's final words of encouragement ringing in his ears: "listen, if it all goes to shit try and get into the cockpit, disable the pilots, set the jet on a collision course with the sea, grab a parachute and bale over the ocean. We'll come and pick you up"

"Really?" Eric asked, enthusiastically

"Not really, no" replied Andy dryly. "If it goes tits up, just stash yourself somewhere and pray to Christ you don't caught"

It was now 7pm. "Wheels up around 9pm", Rachel had told Eric. You need to be on board by 8:15pm to give yourself time to hide before the plane gets too busy". Eric had memorised the outline of the cabin, and tried to visualise it as he walked the mile to the base.

Getting through security at the air base was surprisingly easy. The usual method of entry was to go via the vehicle gate. Wait for a truck to be allowed in and jog in behind it. This always meant Eric had much more space and time than trying to sneak through a pedestrian door. He used this to get all the way to the final hangar which had the president's seal emblazoned on the door as there was no vehicular boom gate to duck under. No-one appeared to be going in or out so he resigned himself to a bit of a wait. He couldn't even see the familiar plane, as it was in the hanger he was now camped outside.

He suddenly heard a thunderous roar above him. Marine One, the president's helicopter, was coming in to land on the other side of the impenetrable wall he was facing. Eric had assumed the president would have driven here, and cursing his luck and the planning department of the British Government. Eric tried to calm his nerves and think of a way through the small door. He paced up and down the length of the hangar trying to come up with something before noticing a small pathway at the far end of the building. Eric quickly walked to it, turning down the path which appeared to head towards the runway. There was no gate at the end of it. It just led straight out to the runway, and there, not one hundred yards in front of him, was the unmistakable sight of Air Force One, clearly not in the hangar as advised.

Behind the plane, Marine One had disgorged its occupants and there were dozens of people running about, talking into their wrists with the other finger pressed into their ears due to the noise of the engines. The President was seemingly already on board, and the cargo doors were very definitely shut tight. 'Oh shit Oh shit Oh shit Oh shit' Eric silently mouthed.

Eric was running towards the plane while trying to come up with yet another Plan B. Two of the biggest Secret Service guards imaginable were standing at the bottom of the famous steps to the door at the front of the aircraft that the president usually appeared out of when arriving in a foreign country, so that route wasn't an option. He skirted under the wing to the other side of the plane - jackpot. The rear steps were there and lots of people were scurrying up and down them holding briefcases, files and guns. This had to be his entry point.

Eric took a deep breath and went for it, bounding up the stairs three at a time. He knew that this would be dangerous but he wasn't going to miss this flight as explaining himself to Andy and Rachel would, frankly, be just embarrassing.

Eric stumbled into the plane. It was a hive of activity, but luckily the corridors were quite wide, so like a footballer dodging tackles he weaved his way forward, making sure he didn't bump into anyone or anything before he found himself at the door of the Presidential suite. The door to the suite was closed. Of course it was.

Eric crouched down in a small alcove next to the door and gulped in deep breaths, trying to calm his breathing, settle his nerves and just take stock of how things were going.

Suddenly, the pilot came over the intercom and announced we were ready to depart, and anyone who didn't want to go to Moscow should fuck off immediately. Those weren't the exact words he used but it seemed to galvanise people into action and less than sixty seconds later half the plane's occupants had disembarked leaving the rest to fasten seatbelts, stow tray tables and take a moment to watch the safety demonstration which involved the head of the Secret Service detail telling everyone to "sit the hell down and buckle the hell up". Eric assumed he had taken this training from EasyJet. Everyone wordlessly sat down and buckled up.

The plane roared into life and galloped down the runway. It took so long to get airborne Eric began to wonder if they were making the entire journey by road, when suddenly Air Force One arched skywards and they were off. 90 seconds later the plane levelled off and the seatbelt sign went off, and everyone was up and about, huddled in earnest meetings, talking on sat phones or getting stuck into the nuts, crisps and coffee.

It wasn't long after take-off that the door to the suite slid open, and the President appeared in the doorway. "Please stay open, please stay open" Eric began to silently chant to himself. He turned left towards his assembled congregation of staff and reporters, resplendent in a bomber jacket and US Air Force captain's baseball cap, and mercifully, the door stayed open.

Eric was in his suite in a flash, assuming he may not have another chance to get in and given the fun day he'd had, absolutely not prepared to miss any more opportunities.

The suite consisted of three main sections. His office, a bathroom and the bedroom. Eric darted past the office and into the bedroom, dropping and rolling as he reached the bed and smacked into a solid frame. There was no gap under the bed for him to hide in. Terrific. This really was going brilliantly. If his luck didn't start changing soon he'd be disabling pilots and baling out over the ocean after all.

Eric went back into the office section of the suite. His laptop was open and his emails and web browser were on display on two large screens on the desk. Eric found an empty chair at the back of the office and sat in it, trying to remain calm and get comfy. Luckily it was made of cloth and not leather so he wouldn't have to peel his sweaty backside off it when the time came.

Only a few minutes later, the President appeared. Followed by his Secretary of Defence, his Environment Minister and the Secretary of State. Eric was no political expert but these were proper players. He counted the number of chairs in the office. Four - including the big one for the main man. Eric was in chair four. The President sat in his, followed by the Defence Secretary and Secretary of State. Eric was firmly boxed in. If he moved, he'd make a sound or bump into one of them. The Environment Secretary moved to Eric's chair and was inches away from sitting on his exposed lap when the President saved his bacon.

"Who the fuck told you to sit, you fucking hippy?" He bellowed. Eric had heard the president speak a few times before. The usual bombast and "thoughts and prayers" shit after yet another mass shooting but this was off the charts. This was a bollocking being given by a master of the art. He shouted "Your policies are awful. Your delivery is weak. And no-one gives a shit about saving the planet if it means taxes have to go up to pay for it".

The President let him have it. Both barrels. The other two Secretaries did what all good teammates do when a colleague is getting a metaphorical kicking. They shrunk into their chairs and pretended to be somewhere else.

Bollocking duly administered, the Environment Secretary wordlessly and brokenly turned and walked out, probably to sit much nearer the back than the front of the plane. The two remaining men were more gently shooed away and Eric and the president were finally alone. He checked his emails, flicked on the TV and then called his personal assistant to bring him his evening meal. This arrived seconds later. A burger and fries and a Diet Coke. He scooped up his laptop and food and padded through to the bedroom, dumping his clothes on the floor and his food and computer on the bedside table before heading to the bathroom. Eric took the opportunity to grab his belt and stash it under his bedside table, and then clicked on the laptop, opening a private browser and quickly navigated to a particularly nasty pornography site and pressed play on the first video that appeared. Eric minimised the window, muted the sound and hoped he wouldn't notice it, and then sat on the floor in the corner and waited, munching on a handful of stolen fries as he did so.

The president appeared a few minutes later. He picked up his burger, put on his bedroom TV and lay back, chomping his food and slurping his drink. He had American football on the telly, so Eric assumed he'd have the duration of the game to wait before he fell asleep, which as he recalled would be a lot of adverts and analysis interspersed with about eight minutes of actual sport. Great.

Within fifteen minutes he was fast asleep. Burger relish on his corpulent stomach and fries scattered on the carpet, and empty paper cup disgorging rapidly melting ice onto the carpet.

Eric decided to wait a little longer before he acted. He assumed if he went too early and he was discovered it would mean he had more chance of being found as well. Eric periodically checked the president's watch, and waited.

When the president's watch read 2am, Eric made his move.

He retrieved the belt from under the bedside table and fed it around the president's neck, gently manoeuvring it into position, pulling the end through the buckle until it was snug. The TV was still blaring, and the football game was still going on. Eric waited until the commentators went absolutely crazy and pulled as hard as he could on the belt.

The President's eyes suddenly popped open. Bulging in his head like a goldfish. He went to open his mouth and that let Eric pull it even tighter. Eric pulled so hard his arms ached. He put a knee on the mattress to give himself additional leverage and pulled again.

The president's eyes searched the room. He looked confused and terrified. He tried to speak but only managed to whisper: "help me, help...me". He clawed at his neck and just managed to hook his thumb under the belt to try and give himself some air, but by then it was far too late.

Eric was pulling so hard on the belt he had no chance of getting any more fingers between it and his neck, and in only a few more seconds he was gone. Unquestionably dead. Even so, Eric held that position for a minute or so, checking his breathing and heart had both absolutely stopped.

Eric then put the laptop on the dead president's stomach, making sure he wiped the belt and PC as best as he could with a presidential towel, before manoeuvring the president's hands all over both. Eric wasn't sure this would make a difference but wanted to feel like he was in control. He definitely wasn't but it seemed to help. The presidential laptop had auto locked but Eric guessed this would be ok as that would add to the story that he'd been there a while if he was found soon afterwards. He placed the free end of the belt into the president's hand. Then he went back to the door of the suite and waited. Eric closed his eyes and took in heavy, deep breaths of oxygen just like Will had taught him.

Eric looked over at the president. It wasn't a particularly edifying image, but that, according to Andy and Rachel, was entirely the point.

Thirty Seven

Eric was suddenly tired. He had no idea what time zone he was in or even where the plane was. He tried to stay awake but as he sat by the door he kept nodding off. He awoke with a start as the sun streamed through one of the windows, and at the sound of a tapping at the door. Eric silently got up and went to sit in a chair in the bedroom.

A voice came from behind the door. "Mr President, your breakfast?". Eric again looked across at the body. It looked perfect. Weird, but exactly as Andy and Rachel had requested.

The door slid open, and the scream that followed filled the plane from front to back, and unleashed hell.

"HELP" screamed his assistant. "SOMEBODY HELP".

Suddenly faces appeared over her shoulder. A tall man in a grey suit and an earpiece pushed past her, causing her to drop the tray and stumble to the floor.

"Lock down. Now" the grey suited man said into his wrist. He sounded calm and collected. "I need the doc here sixty seconds ago" He turned to the assistant who was busy picking up the scattered remnants of the portion of fries and the diet coke cup and plopping them unceremoniously back on the tray. "You. Sit there. Don't move. Speak to no-one. Say nothing". He pointed to a chair in the office. She sat down, dropping the food back on the floor.

Air Force One was put into immediate lockdown. The Presidential suite was sealed. Mr Grey Suit spoke again into his communicator. "I want four Secret Service guards blocking the door. Two on the inside, and two on the outside. No-one in, no-one out. Unless I say so". He didn't wait for an acknowledgment.

Eric knew he had to get out of the suite. He was pretty sure there were no dogs on the plane but couldn't be here if they landed and bought some on.

Another knock on the door. The doctor had appeared and started checking for a pulse. He turned to the man in the suit and said "John, he's dead. He's been dead for a few hours. Look at him John. What the fuck?"

John surveyed the scene. He nodded slowly. "Say nothing Monty. Nothing. Christ, what a mess".

"Say nothing?" replied Monty the doctor. What..."

John cut him off. He turned to the assistant who was still sitting down, eyes wide open and a look of utter shock on her face. "Miss? Go and get yourself a glass of water. Say nothing to anyone. Nothing. Do you understand?". She nodded and sprinted out the door.

"And you two. Outside. Now". The two secret service staff silently exited the room, leaving just John and Monty, and Eric alone with the president's body.

Monty spoke next. "John, what do we do? Look at him. You can see what happened. Jesus Christ. If this gets out we'll be a laughing stock".

John slowly shook his head. "What a mess. Can we say it was a heart attack?" he asked.

Monty replied: "There will be an autopsy. Look at his neck, it'll look like he's been murdered, but we both know what he's done here".

"Ok. We tell the truth. Auto-asphyxiation, I'm guessing? I don't want to think about what's on that laptop. Just confirm the death and I'll deal with the rest".

The doctor checked the pulse and nodded silently to the secret service officer. He spoke into his microphone once more. "Get the secretary of state in here".

Seconds later the secretary appeared. As he did, the doctor covered the president's body with a sheet.

"Sir, the president is dead. I believe we need to get on the ground. Now" said John.

The secretary of state looked bewildered. He nodded, open mouthed. John picked up the telephone on the president's desk and pushed the button to connect him to the pilot. "Land. Now. The Oak has fallen". And he hung up.

It suddenly hit Eric what he'd done. He was shaking now. Not because he'd killed someone - he'd got over that unscrupulous hurdle in Hammersmith -

but it was clear from the panic on everyone's faces that this was utterly seismic. The plane began to descend immediately, and the captain's voice came over the intercom.

"Ladies and Gentlemen, we'll soon be landing for an unscheduled stop in England. Take your seats, fasten your seatbelts and remain in place until you have been given permission to move by the Secret Service".

The plane pitched forward aggressively and nose-dived towards the ground. It landed less than an hour after the pilot's announcement in good old Brize Norton, and as Eric looked out the window he spotted high-viz clad policemen, soldiers, ambulances and blue flashing lights as far as the eye could see. The plane came to a stop at the far end of a runway and the engines were switched off. The doors to the suite were opened and another doctor entered the room and confirmed the President was dead.

John remained in total control. "Get those agents back in here" he barked. As the door slid open Eric could see two agents outside the door as well as the two who had now moved back inside. They were guarding the door and it looked impossible to pass.

John picked up the phone again. He pushed the intercom button and his voice filled the air.

"Everyone is ordered off this aircraft immediately. Leave your bags, papers and cell phones and leave in an orderly fashion, one at a time through the rear doors. The police will escort you to a building where you will be given further instructions".

There was a murmuring from the cabin as people were discussing what was going on. Eric peered out of the window. A funnel of police officers was channelling the passengers and crew down a line towards a hangar. It had started to rain.

The door opened again and a team of forensic officers arrived and started taking photos. They bagged the laptop and belt and the remnants of the burger and fries from the president's dinner. They then checked the body and surrounding areas but didn't get close to Eric who was still sitting in his bedroom chair .

A gurney appeared and they lifted the body onto it, and started to wheel it away. Eric saw his chance and leapt to his feet and followed them out, walking as close to the last forensic officer as he could without bumping into his back.

They march straight past the four security guards, the last of which closed the door behind them. The main door to Air Force One was firmly closed, it appeared the only open door was the one at the back of the plane and fortunately there was no-one guarding those steps. Minutes later Eric was jogging across the tarmac of the RAF base and heading for the security gate on the northern perimeter of the airport.

By now it was 5am and the traffic on the roads was almost non existent. It was raining, windy and freezing cold and Eric knew he had to head back into London and find the Ministry of Defence building that had become his second home before he'd start to feel even remotely safe.

Eric had asked during the planning phase if there would be a rendezvous point. "We have no idea where Air Force One will land" had been Rachel's reply. It could be anywhere in Europe. Or they could turn round and go back to Washington. Get it done and we'll figure something out. Probably".

The word 'probably' was ringing in Eric's ears and he tried to think of what to do next. There were no train stations nearby, so he knew he had a bitch of a walk ahead of him. It was 16 miles to Oxford. Eric figured out which way was East by using his old trick of remembering that Japan was the land of the rising sun and hit the road. The only way to tell where the sun is in an English autumn is to see which clouds are slightly less black and menacing than the rest, so taking a gamble, He picked a direction and started to walk.

Eric had taken no more than five hundred steps when he came across a car in a lay-by with a woman changing a flat tyre. He almost walked right past it when he glanced up and saw the familiar face of Rachel Thomson lugging the spare tyre from the boot. The back door was wide open next to the pavement, not even attracting a moment's suspicion. Jumping in the back with just enough force to make the car rock a little, Eric sat and waited. Rachel didn't flinch, she finished with the tyre, closed the boot with a thump, closed the back door and slid into the driver's seat, before pulling out into the morning's light traffic. She didn't say a word until they hit the A40.

"How's your day been Eric, get up to anything exciting?" She asked

"Oh the usual, almost missed my flight, in-flight service was shit, and worst of all, the telly was stuck on American fucking football". His voice caught on that last word and Eric started sobbing. Actually sobbing. The enormity of what he'd done crashed over him like a tidal wave, and it was a good fifteen minutes before he regained his composure. Rachel sat in studious silence, knowing that he needed to get some emotion out of his system.

Rachel broke the silence in an effort to try and normalise the journey and fill in some gaps. "We left you at Andrews and then got the jet from Washington" she started. We were tracking Air Force One and when it suddenly descended we knew you'd done something. I still can't quite believe you managed to do it Eric, it's remarkable".

"Thanks," mumbled Eric. "I don't supposed you have any clothes for me, do you?". He wasn't in the mood for small talk.

Rachel reached down behind the front passenger seat and pulled out a plastic bag. "Here you go" she smiled.

Eric delved into the bag and pushed his seat back so he had room to pull his tracksuit trousers on and place his hoodie over his head. The seatbelt alarm pinged angrily. He tied his shoes and put his seatbelt back on, allowing the silence to descend once more. Eric spent the rest of the journey reflecting on the events and desperately needing the embrace of his wife. They slipped unnoticed into the underground parking of the Ministry of Defence building.

Thirty Eight

Gloriously, and somewhat unexpectedly given Eric was ready for a full debriefing, Jane was waiting for him. She hugged her husband and kissed him all over. She told him how she knew he'd be doing something big and knew no-one would tell her anyway. Eric assumed she'd guess what he'd been up to as soon as the story broke. Jane was spirited away by Rachel and Will. "Sorry Jane", apologised Will. "We need Eric for some government business".

Back in his suite, Andy Barnes appeared - as always, like a silent ghost. No champagne or cigars, but a welcoming handshake and a "bloody well done". He flicked on the BBC and they sat watching the Vice President taking the vows of office as the official line of "heart-attack, peacefully in his sleep" was trotted out. And that was that.

The following day was spent in Eric's suite with the team holding a thorough debrief on the mission. They paused to watch rolling news reports on the president's demise, including heartfelt eulogies from the presidents of China and Russia. "A man they felt they could do business with" was their repeated line.

There were no rumours about foul play, and certainly none about the manner of his death.

Eric had been over the details a dozen times but was continually questioned on minor points.

"Who was on the plane?"

"Who came into the room after the alarm was raised"

"How long exactly after the body was found did they decide to land?"

"Why did they choose Brize Norton?"

"What time had he pulled the belt tight, and what time did you think he was dead"

At lot of the answers Eric gave were simply "I don't know", and that was the truth.

Eventually, everyone seemed satisfied and as he was on the brink of leaving, Andy pulled Eric to one side. "Eric, I'm really sorry. Something's come up"

"If I cared any less I'd be dead Andy. We have a deal. I'm out. Enough's enough". Eric was calm and assertive.

"You're going to want to hear this Eric, I promise. We're out of ideas and running out of time. We really need your help". It was Andy's turn to sound desperate

"It seems like something is always going to come up. Always. Can't you just let me get on with my life? I have a family and I need to do a lot of making up to them". Eric was starting to get angry now

"Please Eric. Just hear me out, ok?"

Eric nodded, and put his bag down and folded his arms. "You've got five minutes". He said.

Thirty Nine

They climbed the four flights of stairs to the fifth floor of the Ministry of Defence building. Eric hadn't been up here before but this was obviously where some pretty big decisions were made. Thick carpets, paintings of the King and Prime Minister on the walls, enormous secretaries' desks outside huge office doors, all of which were closed except for the very last one at the end of the main corridor. Andy led Eric to the far end of the table and motioned for him to sit, while he took the chair at the head of the table.

Eric turned to find a dozen soldiers staring at him. Most were opened mouthed.

Andy spoke. "Eric, meet some of the lads from the 21st SAS. Lads, meet Eric. In case you hadn't guessed, he's the invisible bloke I've been telling you about".

Eric nodded a genial hello and then realised none of them could see his head move. He squeaked a rather pathetic "hi guys". He received twelve curt synchronised nods of welcome back. Eric had spent time around a few US secret service officers on Air Force One, and in the White House, but none of them scared him shitless like this lot. Even the nods of welcome were menacing. They were all different heights, builds, races and ages but the eyes were all identical. Cold, hard, judging. And not impressed by what they were looking at, clearly. It took more than an invisible man in a tracksuit to impress these fuckers, he could tell.

"Now", Andy went on. "Eric, tell me what you know about Prince Albert".

"Well, I don't have one, but I accept everyone in this room's right to mutilate their bodies in any way they see fit" Eric stammered. Totally perplexed at the question. Hilarity ensued. The SAS clearly thought this was the stupidest thing they'd heard all year and began cackling at the insanity of Eric's answer.

"Silence". Whispered Andy, barely audible over the din. Silence he got. "This is not a fucking joke". Twelve suitably chastened men stared down at the table in front of them. Andy was in terrifying form. Eric felt like a tit and his face flushed with embarrassment. Thank Christ they couldn't see me.

"Not **A** Prince Albert. **The** Prince Albert".

A screen whirred down from the ceiling behind Andy. A light flicked on and the screen was filled with the image of a small child aged around 6, beaming at the camera and dressed in a sailor's uniform. Andy continued to speak.

"Prince Albert. Fourth in line to the throne. Seven years old next Saturday. Only son of the Duke and Duchess of Dorset, goes to school at Westminster Prep and is the King's favourite Great Grandson".

"The only people who know the details of what I am about to tell you are the Prince's parents, his security detail, the Prime Minister and the fourteen of us in this room".

Eric realised that the five minutes he'd offered Andy were up. But he also knew he wasn't going home today.

"Four days ago, the Prince was at school as normal. As always, he was accompanied by his close protection officer who sits and waits for him in the school office until he finishes for the day, checking in on him every thirty minutes. The Prince excused himself and went to the bathroom during a lesson, and disappeared. The protection officer noticed he was missing no more than ten minutes after he was last seen, and locked down the building. We have since established that a janitor had been waiting in the bathroom and as the Prince entered he was bound, gagged and bundled into a laundry basket and wheeled out of the school through the service entrance and into a waiting van with false plates. Extensive checks have confirmed the janitor who has worked at the school for ten years has disappeared without a trace and we believe he is overseas with a fat pile of cash. He is not our concern now. He'll be found and dealt with in good time. We tracked the van to an underground car park at a Southampton shopping centre and unsurprisingly it was discovered empty with no fingerprints or DNA to be found. The trail went cold for twenty four hours, and then we received this":

The screen flickered and a video replaced the smiling Prince. A balaclava-clad man was sitting behind a plain wooden desk, in a plain brick windowless room. He was also dressed in army fatigues but without the poise, grace or muscles of the men Eric was sitting with. He began to speak. He had a heavy accent. Italian? Spanish? He wasn't great at identifying them, but then he realised he should probably be listening to what he had to say than figuring out which football team he supported.

"Good day to you, my British friends" the accented man began. Italian. Definitely Italian. "By now you will be frantically searching for your young Prince. I am here to tell you he is quite safe, and quite well. He is a charming boy. The birthmark under his right armpit is very small but doesn't distract from his handsome face, I am sure you will agree". Eric stiffened, and turned his body to look at Andy. He nodded back, affirmation that this guy wasn't bluffing. "Now. We know little Albert here is a billionaire many times over, and all we really want is one of those billions. Just one. If not, he'll be posted back to you in a billion little boxes. So. We'll give you until noon on Wednesday to transfer the money in equal parts to the dozen account numbers we sent with this transmission. Once received, we'll let you know where he is and you can come and get him. Goodbye".

And with that the screen went black. The room was in silence. Andy just let the words permeate into everyone's brain. No-one spoke for what seemed an eternity. Finally, one of the soldiers raised a hand. "What's the plan then boss?"

As usual, Andy had one.

Forty

Andy clicked a pointer which was aimed at the screen. A map of Southern Italy appeared in. "We've traced the accent to the region of Calabria in Sicily. Everything points to the Sicilian Mafia. They certainly have the balls, the infrastructure and the network to pull off something so incredible, and they still practically own Sicily". Another click, and the map zoomed into the island at the bottom of the Italian boot. "Sure, they have had a significantly reduced influence over the past decade or so but this would give them new status and leverage in Europe and enough capital to expand their operation globally. We have spent hours reviewing satellite imagery and finally been able to track a small fishing boat from Southampton which had slipped out under cover of darkness on the night of the kidnapping and travelled across the channel to Cherbourg. The occupants were then traced via security cameras driving through the night and following day down to Naples, where they boarded a ferry to Palermo. The van has been spotted parked outside a farmhouse in the hills near Marianopoli, and it was almost certain that this is the balaclava-man made his film".

Eric didn't question how they obtained this knowledge, or this footage. But he had a gnawing certainty in the pit of his stomach that he was about to be sent to Italy.

Andy continued: "the Italian government are not aware of the kidnapping and what we are about to attempt will have absolutely no chance of success if we had to jump through a bunch of diplomatic hoops. We also can't be sure someone won't tip the Mafiosi off about our arrival. It has to be assumed that the Prince is currently with balaclava-man, and that's where we are heading. Secrecy is key gentlemen".

Silence again filled in the room. The soldiers' stares never left Andy's face.

"Plans are being drawn up to transfer the money in case things go tits up. The palace has managed to bury the story, saying Prince Albert has been feeling unwell and was found in the playground by a policeman who drove him home where he is having bed rest on doctor's orders. The press hasn't even had a whiff of the news and that's the way it is going to stay. Questions?"

There were no questions.

Forty One

An hour later and all fourteen men were stepping out of a helicopter at Brize Norton, and onto a waiting Gulfstream jet. The stairs were hoisted up, the doors closed and they were off. By now it was early evening and the full briefing started in earnest. The SAS had bought very little in the way of equipment. A few rucksacks and crates had been loaded into the hold, but nothing else.

"Your job Eric is to provide intel on what's going on inside the building". Andy was calm, and measured. He continued "How many men? Which ones are armed? Which rooms are they in? And of course, is the Prince even there? Find that out, come back to me and tell me everything. No detail will be insignificant, I promise you that".

They studied photos of the building and Eric was told in no uncertain terms not to engage anyone. Sneak in, have a look about, sneak out, tell the lads with the biceps what was what and keep your head out of the way of the ensuing carnage. That suited Eric just fine.

The briefing finished. Eric sat back in his seat gazing out of the window into the darkness below, hoping to focus on the job in hand. He started to visualise the layout of the house and as he did so the mocking abuse from the soldiers began.

"So how many banks have you robbed you thieving bastard?"

"I reckon you're really bloody ugly and went invisible on purpose"

"Bet you miss your cosy little call centre now eh?"

"Is your cock was invisible too?" Eric finally bit back with the age old "ask your Mum" which in hindsight was a mistake.

Eric had assumed that they would enjoy getting some reciprocal abuse to prove his confidence, but they didn't. He was pelted with shoes and lever-arch files and anything they could get their hands on.

"Permission requested to chuck this cheeky fucker out the plane boss".

"Denied" replied Andy, without even looking up from his folder. .

The team had been briefed on who Eric was, and how he's been working for the government for a while now.

"So was that you with president on Air Force One? I bet it was" said one. The squad had put two and two together and landed on four, and they knew it.

"It's ok, you can tell us. Andy told us it was you, just give us the details"

Andy looked up from his papers

"Sorry lads, nothing to do with me. I was on holiday" replied Eric. Andy went back to his scribbling.

"We'll make you an honorary member of the SAS if you just admit what you've done". Pleaded another

As instructed, Eric denied everything.

"What about that weird ISIS camp commander. That was you, wasn't it? Asked a third.

To Eric's relief, Andy stood up and finally intervened. "Eric can tell you, but then he'd have to kill you. All of you." This was met with howls of derision.

Gradually the piss-taking eased and as the plane approached Italy people started to focus on the job at hand the soldiers started to lose themselves in their thoughts.

Andy explained "My cover is that I am flying in as a tourist for a few days on my private jet. The Italians won't let a plane land unless someone gets off and clears immigration, and if they see this lot barrelling towards customs we won't get very far" He nodded in the direction of the squad. "You'll meet me outside the airport. I've arranged some transport so keep your head down and follow the lads"

They landed in Palermo at dusk. Sicily seemed dark and foreboding beyond the fence, and Eric shivered, knowing there were some right evil bastards lurking in the hills. He turned to see his new mates all unpacking the crates and rucksacks and soon they were brandishing machine guns and balaclavas which were all rolled up like beanies on top of their heads. They disembarked and stood on the runway behind the plane, out of sight of the small airport terminal. In a flash one of the lads had sliced through the fence and they were out by the main airport service road. Ten minutes later Andy appeared in a large hired minivan and everyone piled in and headed into the hills.

The grim silence that had first greeted Eric in the top floor boardroom of the MOD building that morning had returned. The piss taking and bonhomie that had been so evident on the plane was a distant memory. Andy drove the last twenty minutes or so at a snail's pace with the lights off. Keeping the van in first or second gear and never revving the engine. All windows were open so they could listen out for any noise and as they neared the target he sent two men out to walk ahead to find a place to hide the van, which they soon did in a small gap in the trees. The rest of the journey would be on foot, and in silence.

All the men were carrying machine guns moving quickly and silently along the side of the narrow road. The first man stopped and squatted down and immediately everyone did the same. Except Eric.

He was halfway down the column and didn't see the order to stop being given and crashed straight into the man in front of him, losing his balance and toppling into the road. It was like bouncing off a rock. Eric was dragged back into line and the age old wanker hand signal was given to him by the lump of granite he'd bumped into. It was hard to see in the darkness. The moon was a small crescent but gave off just enough light to see a few yards ahead. They crouch walked the next 200 yards and there was the farmhouse, almost hidden through the trees, a single light flickering from a ground floor window.

Andy came back to Eric's position in the line and whispered for him to strip. Eric did as he was told and started slowly creeping towards the farmhouse. His feet sounded loud on the gravel so he tried to tiptoe as quietly as he could. He crept up to the front door as instructed and began to circle the building, looking for either a way in, or a window he could peak through. He started to move around the building clockwise, passing numerous darkened windows and closed doors. The light they could see was the hallway, and the clouded window of the front door didn't let Eric make any judgements of who was inside.

"I can't see anyone, or anything. The house sounds empty. The light is in the hallways but everything else is in total darkness. There's no-one watching us through windows as far as I can tell". Eric whispered in Andy's ear.

"The plan is the plan. Go back. See if any doors are unlocked. If they are, go in. You need to get inside and check what's happening" Andy's voice was calm and measured.

Eric's heart sank. The house seemed empty, he'd done what he had been asked to do. "Andy, the place is deserted, I'm sure it's fine"

"Someone switched that light on Eric. Go and find out who. I'm not asking". Eric was terrified but Andy didn't hesitate. "Just be quiet and keep low. We're all here and we have your back. Now go"

Eric went back round the building and found the door again. He spent a good five minutes standing next to it, calming his breathing down like he'd been shown how to do, listening for sounds. None came. He turned the handle and the door gently, and silently, started to swing open. He inched it ajar, just wide enough for him to slip inside. He pulled it almost closed behind him.

The room was in total darkness. Eric could just see a slither of light coming from under a door at the far side of the room. He guessed this would lead to the hallway. He turned to check door behind him appeared closed and walked over to the light, feeling his way around a table and chairs and pressed his ear to the door. No sounds. He turned the handle and gently pushed the door open. It opened a few inches before the hinges started squealing angrily. Eric immediately stopped and held his breath. There were no angry shouts or lights being turned on. Just the sound of his heart hammering in his ears. He pushed the door as slowly as he could until there was a big enough gap for him to squeeze through. Eric decided to leave it open for his impending exit and took the chance it wouldn't be noticed. The shift from dark room to bright hallway took some adjustment. There was a closed door ahead of him, and a flight of stairs that led down to a cellar to his right. Eeny, Meeny, Miny, Mo. He picked the cellar.

Eric tiptoed down the concrete steps and could make out a flickering light near the bottom. He crept down to where the ground floor ended to create the cellar ceiling and paused, crouching down to see who was there. It was a large, open plan room with a candle on a small table in the middle. There were four camp beds at one end, three of which held a sleeping occupant. There was a fourth man sitting by the candle in an armchair, rifle across his lap. His eyes were closed and his head was back. He looked fast asleep and was snoring gently. Eric could just make out a door at the far end of the room, so, as quietly as possible, he walked down the last remaining stairs and headed for it.

Eric tiptoed over the stone floor to the door and peeked inside. Jackpot. There, handcuffed to a bed, blindfolded and gagged was a small child, dressed in a school uniform but sitting up in bed and gently sobbing. Eric had this idea that if he found him he could carry him past any sleeping guards to safety but now he was in the room with him that seemed fanciful at best. He'd almost certainly cry out and

Eric wasn't sure which was easier, breaking open his handcuffs with his bare hands or carrying the whole bed out past the guards with him on sitting silently on top. 'No Eric', he told himself. 'Follow the plan'.

He retraced his steps, making mental notes of the position of each man, the weapons they had by their sides, the exit route – all like he was instructed. Back up the stairs, through the hallway, through the darkened room and out into the fresh air. Eric breathed a huge sigh of relief. 'I'm the man' he whispered to himself. 'I. Am. The. Man'.

"You really are a fucking idiot" hissed Andy in a furious whisper. "Who's behind the doorway in the room at the top of the stairs? How many armed men are in there, just waiting for us?"

Eric's face flushed. He'd forgotten to check behind that door in his haste to get back and share his news.

There was some furious whispered debate about what to do. Go in, deal with the 4 in the cellar and handle anyone in the unchecked room as and when that happened, or send Eric back in to check again. It was 3am. Sunrise was in 2 hours. Any further delays could risk people waking up and then they'd be in the shit.

Andy gathered everyone around. "We go in together. Curtis, you're up front holding this pen torch so we can follow you. The light is barely visible but we'll know where you are and will be close behind. Give signals based on what you are encountering ahead. Steady light, we'll follow. One flash, we wait. Two flashes, we shoot everyone. Just hit the deck as you flash twice or you'll be torn in half. We'll aim above knee height so stay low till it's over"

"Thanks lads, appreciated". Eric wasn't sure if this was sarcasm or true appreciation but nervous energy was coursing through his veins.

"Oh", Andy continued, "if the bad guys are all sleeping or looking the other way, go a few metres ahead of us and try and lift all the weapons from the cellar out of the way before giving the signal. Half the men will follow you down, the other half will wait by the mystery door and see what comes out of it. Understood?"

Everyone understood. The sudden sound of twelve weapons being checked and loaded sounded unfeasibly loud to Eric, and silence descended again.

So back in they went. Eric, leading the way, he pushed the back door open, making sure the feeble light from his torch was showing behind him so the men could follow. He got to the squeaky door and very, very slowly pushed it open. It complained again but he managed to get it just over halfway ajar which he figured would be enough for some of the larger lads to get through without a struggle. Eric crept down the stairs, six very heavily armed men moving soundlessly behind him

As he reached the point of no return Eric scanned the cellar room again. Four camp beds, three sleeping men filling them. But this time, the chair by the candle was empty.

The rifle that had been on the sleeping man's lap was propped up against the chair but he was nowhere to be seen. The far door to the room that housed the Prince was now wide open.

Eric stopped. He needed the men behind him to stop. Brain fog. Was it one flash, or two? Christ. Such a simple instruction. Eric replayed the moment Andy had said it earlier. He just couldn't remember this basic detail. He could sense the men tensing behind him. One flash. Was it? Probably. Oh well, one way to find out. Eric rolled the dice and flashed the torch once and ducked, just in case. Nothing happened. He exhaled and went downstairs. As he reached the bottom he looked back up the steps and could just make out a pair of SAS eyes watching him, waiting for the signal. You wouldn't have seen him if you didn't know he was there.

Eric reached the far door and peered inside. There was guard number four. Sitting on the bed with the Prince. He was taking a selfie on his phone with his bound and gagged captive, grinning like a man who believed he was about to be rich. Eric quickly nipped back into the main room, picked up the guard's rifle and tiptoed around the other camp beds, scooping up the guns as instructed. He placed them under the steps in the darkness, again, as instructed. He went back into the Prince's bedroom, made sure he had clean line of sight to his friendly eyes on the stairs and pointed the torch at him. Steady light from the torch pointing right back up the steps. Then one flash. Wait.

Eric got within a yard of the guard who was sitting on the bed. He opened his free hand and, as shown to him during his time back in the MOD basement, slapped the unsuspecting guard hard across the side of his head catching him full on the ear. Far more effective than an uppercut, and more disabling than a kick to the nuts, he had been assured. Somehow, it worked. As he recoiled in utter shock Eric flashed the light twice and jumped onto the bed, holding Prince Albert as tightly as he could while covering his ears. The noise that followed was deafening, but mercifully it only lasted a few seconds. The unmistakable sound of three very loud, very angry double taps from the next room, followed by two more a just few yards away. The smell of cordite hung in the air. It was all over.

Torches appeared and swept the room. One of the soldiers pulled some bolt cutters from his belt and deftly clipped the handcuffs open. Another soldier picked the young prince up and sprinted out the room, up the stairs and straight out the front door.

"I'm fine", squeaked Eric, to no-one in particular. No response.

Everyone followed Albert's backside as it was hoisted hastily up the steps. As they got to the hallway Eric saw the mystery door. It was wide open and as he glanced inside he recognised the table and brick wall from the ransom video. No-one appeared to be lurking in there and he wasn't going to wait to find out. Eric ran out with the rest of the men all the way back to the waiting van, Andy behind the wheel, engine running. They climbed in and were away, this time with the lights on and no concerns about a revving engine or squealing tyres.

Andy screamed around corners and tore along the windy backroads all the way to Palermo. Prince Albert sat, quietly crying. His blindfold and gag removed his eyes were wide at the sight in front of him. He was in the arms of an SAS soldier who was whispering soothing words of comfort in his ear.

Eric leaned back in his seat. "Can someone throw me my clothes? He asked.

"Sorry mate, we left them in the farmhouse with your name and address scrawled in them" shouted one to general laughter.

Eric got up, found his clothes and got dressed. They raced back to the airport, squeezed through the gap and were airborne before the smell of gunpowder had left the farmhouse.

They landed at Brize Norton, there were the Duke and Duchess, and the reunion between them and their son was one of those moments Eric would never forget. They were whisked into a VIP lounge and the SAS stood around and chatted with royalty like they'd probably done many times before. Eric overheard plenty of industrial language that made them roar with laughter, and no doubt some relief. Eric wasn't sure if he was supposed to be part of this. He didn't know who was allowed to know about him, so he found an empty chair in the corner and tried to blend into the background.

Forty Two

Twenty minutes later, the room was cleared and the royals were on their way back to their palace. The soldiers had all disappeared into a waiting helicopter to be taken back to their base in London. Only Andy and Eric remained.

"Thank you Eric", said Andy. "Thank you for everything"

Eric suspected a 'but' was coming. He was wrong.

"That's it. You're free to go. The money is yours. The slate is wiped clean. Will is bringing the car round now. He'll take you home. Jane and the kids are there now. They're expecting you".

Eric was stunned. Free? Really?

Andy continued "Keep your head down. Keep your mouth shut. If the world knew about you, life would become unbearable. We'll deny you even exist of course, but you'll need to figure the rest out yourself. Good luck, and don't keep in touch"

Andy stood and thrust his arm out. Eric stood and ignored it, choosing a bear hug instead that took the MI6 man by surprise. "Alright you big softy, bugger off. Go and be happy".

"One last thing" Said Eric. This invisibility. Any idea if it will wear off? Any cure you guys can help me out with?"

"Thought you'd ask" replied Andy softly. "No. Afraid not. We have a team of people looking at it but nothing yet. It really is the darndest thing. Look, if anything changes I'll call you, I owe you that much".

This hit Eric hard. He wanted his life back. That's all he wanted now.

On cue Will stuck his head round the door. "Taxi sir?". Eric slowly followed him to the waiting Range Rover and climbed in.

Eric arrived home to hugs and kisses and a Chinese takeaway. His first family meal in his own house for as long he could remember. He listened as the kids shared stories of their recent school days and the life he'd been missing while he was away. More pangs of regret.

As they cleared away the plates and containers and packed the kids to bed, Jane spoke. "We need a holiday. As a family. A proper one".

"How on earth can we go on holiday with me like this?" argued Eric.

"We could drive somewhere? Or you could meet us on the bike?" Jane replied

"And how am I getting through customs?" Eric asked. "Unless you want to spend two weeks in Weymouth every year with me sneaking about trying not to bump into people. Do you know how hard that is? Or I could dress like a burns victim. How about that?

Jane held her husband's hand. "I'm sorry. I just want us to be a normal family again. Go to bed, I'll wash up here"

Eric's mood darkened as he climbed the stairs. He hadn't been in his house since he'd been snatched by MI6 and he shivered as he glanced at the front door. So much had changed since he left the house that day. He straightened a picture on the wall. It was one of the family he'd taken with Jane's camera that he'd developed with the chemicals that had made him invisible. He traced the outline of his own face with his finger. A face he hadn't seen for months. A face he missed.

Eric woke the next morning. It was grey and overcast. He wandered downstairs. Jane had returned to her job in the shelter, bored from being at home all day and needing something worthwhile to do. The kids were at school. Eric flicked on the TV.

Coverage of the preparations for the president's funeral were on all the news channels. Images of his mourning wife were everywhere. She was smiling quite happily while dressed in black and Eric raised his coffee mug in a silent salute as she appeared on the screen. 'You're welcome' he said aloud to no-one.

Eric wandered to the garage. He considered taking his bike for a ride but couldn't find the energy. He scrolled through the channels, finding the same American sitcom he'd watched in Washington just days ago and settling down for a day on the couch. He picked at the leftover Chinese. He drank more coffee. He dozed on the couch and mindlessly flicked through channels for the rest of the day.

He repeated this routine for a week. The highlight was the kids getting home from school. He'd help with their homework and prepare the evening meal, then settle down with Jane to watch more TV before heading to bed. Eric was slowly going out of his mind with boredom.

The weekend was worse. He was a prisoner in his own house. His friends hadn't called to invite him to the pub, and even his brother didn't call or message. He felt alone and depressed. He couldn't go out and the walls of the house felt like they were closing in. He kept checking his phone. No calls or texts in over a week. Just emails from Nigerian princes needing to move money offshore. He was almost tempted to reply just to have someone to talk to. The juxtaposition of his new boring life against the excitement of working for the government jarred. He found himself longing to be Mr Average again.

On Sunday morning, his phone rang.

"Eric?" called Jane, walking in from the kitchen and clutching his phone. "It's Rachel, she's asking for you".

"Am I not allowed to even answer my own phone any more?" snapped Eric.

"Just talk to her, she sounds excited" replied his wife, ignoring the barb.

Eric looked at the phone. He wanted something to do, but working undercover for the government was not it.

"Hey Eric, I've got a surprise for you. Jump on the bike, come down to the Ministry of Defence building this afternoon. Bring Jane. I promise you'll like it".

Eric considered this for a moment. Red pill or blue pill? Stay or go? It was Rachel's unusual infectious excitement that made him choose.

"Come on Jane" said Eric with a grin. "One more adventure".

Forty Three

They arrived at the MoD, and again were ushered through security Rachel took Jane and Eric through some underground passages that he had never encountered before, into what appeared to be some kind of laboratory. At the far end of the lab there were a couple of men in white coats who were almost cartoonish in their similarity to how Eric imagined mad scientists to look. Both men had glasses, bald patches and goofy grins that suggested they were in on some superbly clever joke that no-one else was intelligent enough to understand. As they walked in, they both looked up with huge smiles on their faces. It was endearing and creepy in equal measure.

Eric was still wearing his motorbike balaclava and sunglasses so looked relatively human, but as they entered the room Rachel nodded at him to take them off, which he felt always made him look a little like the headless horseman.

"Jane, what's going on?" asked Eric. Jane just squeezed Eric's hand and smiled.

Eric pulled off his headgear. "Hello, I'm Eric" he said, walking towards the two men.

"Oh, we know exactly who you are Eric" said the first man. "I'm professor Jim Baker, it's an absolute pleasure to meet you. A real pleasure". He shook Eric's proffered hand with great excitement and pointed to his colleague and said "and this is Professor Silas Ferguson, and we've been working on something for you for the past few months. It really is a pleasure to finally meet you as we've been fingering your face for quite some time". They both sniggered at this joke a little longer than was comfortable, but Eric laughed along in nervous anticipation.

Professor Baker pulled a small suitcase out from under his desk. The grin on his face widening like he was a magician about to deliver the amazing reveal of an impossible trick to a bamboozled child. Eric half expected him to ask him if this was his card when he thumbed open the two latches and opened the lid.

What he pulled out was white cylinder which looked to Eric like a can of fly spray, "Here", he said. "Roll up your sleeve". Eric turned to look at Rachel, and then Jane. Both nodded encouragement.

Eric rolled up his sleeve and pushed his arm towards Professor Baker.

Baker took Eric's arm in his free hand, shook the can vigorously and sprayed a pale pink mist over the invisible skin.

"Christ that's hot" exclaimed Eric, trying to pull his arm away. But the grip was too strong.

"Look" said Jane. Her eyes widening in delight

Eric looked down. He could see his arm. "What the...."

"We think we matched your skin tone", began Ferguson. It's taken a while. It's a little warm at first due to the bonding it has to do with your skin, but it cools soon enough.

Eric stared at his arm. "do my hand", he instructed

Baker shook the can again and sprayed Eric's hand, the mist landing on his palm and making it appear as if by magic. "Tada!" said the professor.

Rachel clapped her hands with glee. "It works. I knew it would"

Eric ripped his jacket and t-shirt off. "Keep going", he begged.

"This way", said professor Ferguson, and led Eric to a large tube that was standing in the corner of the lab. "Now get undressed and pop these on", he instructed. Eric put the two eye protectors he had been handed in place. "That's it, now step inside". Eric did as he was told. "This is going to be a little uncomfortable, but it'll be over in thirty seconds, I promise. Just keep your mouth closed until the door opens."

Eric stepped inside. The door closed behind him and he was in darkness. The sound of hissing and the faint smell of solvent filled his senses. The hot mist pricked at his skin and the odour almost made him gag. Then it stopped and the door opened. Eric picked the eye protectors from his face and let his vision adjust to the light.

Eric stepped outside and turned to look at Jane. She was staring at her husband, opened mouthed. "What?" he asked, inquisitively.

Jane pointed at a mirror on the wall. "Go see for yourself, handsome", she instructed. He walked over to the mirror, and there, staring back at him, for the first time in months was the face of Eric Curtis.

Eric stared at his reflection. Bald, and with no eyes or eyebrows but unmistakably him. He looked down and saw his body. He immediately put his hands over his privates before he turned round and faced the room. "I'd shake your hands, but you know.." he gestured downwards. "Can I put some clothes on please?"

Jane tossed him his t-shirt and jeans and he dressed quickly.

"Look, this is amazing" said Eric. "But the eyes are still a bit of a giveaway".

Professor Baker stepped forward. He pulled a small case from his pocket and opened a selection of coloured contact lenses. Eric selected a pair of brown ones and used the mirror to slot them in, blinking as he did so. He looked at his reflection. It was him.

Eric turned to the team. "You could have given me some bloody hair" he laughed. Rachel took her cap off, loosened the strap and handed it to Eric.

He put it on and looked in the mirror again. He looked boringly normal, and Eric hadn't never been as happy to be so.

Professor Baker walked out with them. "This skin replicator is pretty hard wearing, but we don't have a huge amount lying about so look after it Eric" he explained. "Try and avoid cuts and grazes or it'll start to look really odd. It's made of the same stuff you had your stomach sprayed with when you first came in here. It will wash off with that special soap, do you remember?"

"I do" replied Eric, "can I have some?"

"Whatever for?" replied Baker.

"Well, in case..." Eric stopped. "You're right. You keep it. I won't be needing it".

"Thought not" the professor said. "Now, this is something we can manufacture although it is still something of a prototype, but now we know it works we'll make more and you just let us know if it starts to fall apart. We'll keep some in reserve so you can go out in public and enjoy life again. Apparently the country owes you a debt of gratitude so we're happy to help". This was the first time Eric really considered that he'd been doing a reasonable job for his country since he'd incapacitated the leader of the opposition, so it was nice to get a little bit of feedback on his performance.

"Is there anyone working on a permanent cure?" Eric asked. The professors gave each other and Rachel nervous glances.

"Rachel?". Eric prayed she was about to say yes. She didn't.

"Goodbye Eric. It's been a pleasure working with you. Maybe our paths will cross again. Who knows?" Rachel hugged Eric and stepped back. "Keep the hat. It suits you".

They raced home on the bike. Eric was grinning from ear to ear.

Epilogue

They went out to the Chinese restaurant for dinner and fizzy drinks that night, staying out until well past midnight. It was the family's first proper family night out months and they had a blast. When they got home they stayed up playing music and laughing like a proper family you see on those frozen food adverts on the telly. Eric told the kids they had that evening to ask him anything about what he'd been up to and he'd be totally honest with them

"Dad, Did you meet anyone famous?"

"No comment"

"Did you steal anything?"

"No comment"

"Did you do anything we would have read about in the papers?"

"No comment"

"Dad, Was the president dying anything to do with you?

"You're being silly now. Off to bed. Night kids, love you"

"Love you Dad, night Mum".

And they scarpered up the stairs. Jane looked at Eric quizzically. "*Was* the president dying anything to do with you?"

Eric laughed. "Jane, I've being doing really boring stuff. It didn't involve murdering the president and making it look like suicide!"

"I thought he had a heart attack?!" Said Jane.

"Night Jane, off to bed. Love you" said Eric.

The next morning they had a family breakfast. "Right", announced Eric. "The government paid me pretty well for the work I did and your Mum and I think we all deserved a treat".

The gambling money they had earned was sitting in the bank account, all nice and legal. The mortgage had been paid off with over half of it, but they still had a hundred thousand pounds left over. "Tell me one thing each of you wants".

Oscar went first: "I want a guitar"

"Done" Said Eric. "Kate, what about you?"

Kate thought for a minute. "A holiday. Somewhere sunny where we can all sit on the beach together like a normal family"

"Perfect" replied Eric. "You pick somewhere and we'll book it today. That's a great idea. You get to choose, ok?"

Kate squealed with delight.

"Jane? How about you?".

"A hot tub and a sauna. And an outside shower"

The kids thought this was an amazing idea.

Eric reached for his laptop. He had some shopping to do. As he started googling musical instruments, holidays and hot tubs, Jane blocked him. "What about you darling? What do you want". Jane expected him to reply that he had all he wanted, right there. But he didn't.

"A Porsche 911". He replied, without hesitation. Jane groaned.

Eric spent the next hour ordering the hot tub, sauna and guitar from the internet, and left Kate to book the holiday. He grabbed Jane and said "come on, we're going to the dealership".

They jumped on Eric's bike and headed to the West London Porsche garage to buy Eric's dream car. When they arrived, he sat in the blue 911 he'd always lusted after and felt the German workmanship envelop him. Fortunately, it was a different car to the one he'd borrowed previously, with that particular car conspicuous by its absence. Eric asked for the key, and started the engine, revving the accelerator like a 17 year old boy racer and causing the staff in the showroom to cover their ears. As he stepped out he looked up and saw the unmistakable face of Kenny Sinclair staring at him.

His old Finance Director from the call centre. He of the shitty keyboard and perma-angry demeanour. He looked surprised that Eric would even be in this dealership, let alone considering buying a car.

"Robbed a bank, have you Eric?" He asked. Eric began thinking of ways to placate him and justify his actions like he always used to do on those weekly zoom calls, when it dawned on him that he was a very different person now.

"Hello Kenny", Eric beamed. "Great to see you. How's business?" This caught his old nemesis off guard.

Eric then realised he wasn't scared any more. He didn't really care what Kenny thought of him. He didn't care what anyone thought of him. He was proud to be Eric Curtis. And if people didn't like it, fuck them.

"Actually", said Kenny. "The India move has been cancelled. It's all gone tits up. And to make matters worse, your replacement left a month ago. Couldn't handle the pressure. I'm glad I've bumped into you. Your name came up in last week's board meeting. We could really use your help. How do you fancy coming back? It'd obviously mean more money, and a better parking space. You interested?"

Eric thought for a minute. "I'll be honest Kenny, the job was fine. You were just very, very difficult to work with. I hated it. I felt like a nobody. If you promise to support me and my team, and learn to talk to people like they matter, then I'm interested".

"Great news", said Kenny, "everyone will be thrilled to have you back. I'll send over some paperwork tomorrow. Sinclair shook Eric by the hand and headed for the door.

Eric got back in the car he wanted so badly. As he did the dealership manager came over and Eric said "Let me have your bank details so I could transfer the cash immediately". The dealer beamed with delight. Eric sat, feeling very pleased with himself. As he did, he looked to the right and caught a sight of his reflection in the window of the showroom. A middled aged man in a convertible.

"Jesus, I look like a twat" He said, loud enough for some of the staff and customers to look round.

Eric got out of the car, made his apologies and left. He had a nice car. He didn't need to draw this level of attention to himself. He didn't need a Porsche to fill a void in his life. Not anymore.

It's been a year since Eric Curtis last spoke to Rachel or Andy. A year of hot tubs, holidays, dog walks and family takeaways. A year where Eric got promoted at work. A year where he is seen, everywhere he goes. A year of being fulfilled, and a year of being happy with what he has.

He still checks his phone every few hours or so. He always makes sure it's fully charged.

Just in case.

Printed in Great Britain
by Amazon